It's The Holidays

Breaking Rules Publishing
Short Story Book Project

Published By
Breaking Rules Publishing

Soft Cover - 10778
Published by Breaking Rules Publishing
Pompano Beach, FL
www.breakingrulespublishing.com

Acknowledgment

Thank you to all the writers that have supported Breaking Rules Publishing. Especially those that have submitted and been placed within this anthology.

Well done.

Story Table

Hen Spawn
by Terry Groves

Christmas lights twinkled along the edge of the saggy roof. Someone had even worked to extend the line of Christmas cheer to the unpainted barn that stood behind the lonely looking house, but the string had come up short, ending three feet from the eaves. Inside the barn, a tarry mass clung to the underside of the roof, vibrating with the effort of hanging there. Winter's chill bit through the tin roof, coaxing condensation to form where the dark shape made contact with the ceiling. Sticky tendrils found purchase in cracks, as It pressed itself into more holds. It continued studying the small figure that squatted four feet below.

Ryan hunched over his work. The canvas of his heavy coat rasped as he moved his arms. The dust and smells of the straw filled loft were as familiar as the aroma of his grandmother's Christmas baking. He squinted at his task. With the concentration of a surgeon but the curiosity of a eight-year-old, he removed another limb from a long-legged spider. He was lost to the real world, focused on the latest twitching appendage as he dropped it by the others on the straw-littered, loft floor. Some of the had stopped moving already. They didn't kick as long in the cold.

Ryan didn't see the black, needle thin finger that stretched out of the shadows above him. It arrowed closer, slowing as It approached his toque covered head. It hovered a moment, debating its next action. Then, with an eerie speed, It darted and touched the boy on the back of the neck.

Ryan yelped, snapping his hand to his injury, barely missing the tendril as It pulled back into the shadows above. Ryan looked around to see what had stung him, tears blurring his vision. Sobbing, he scrambled out of the loft, scattering chickens in the coop at the bottom of the ladder. His neck hurt with the fury of a bee sting but there shouldn't be any this time of year. He ran the short distance to the house so his grandmother could fuss over the small boil that had bubbled on his neck.

It was hungry and It was cold. The temperature didn't bother It much, but hunger could drive It out into the open where It was vulnerable. It had dared to taste the child, had It not? That had been foolish. Straw prickled but was a minor distraction against the hunger that was becoming consuming. It would have chuckled at the pun if It had the ability to laugh.

Too much time had passed since that last rat had burrowed right to it, under the straw. Raising itself, It formed a tunnel for the rat to enter and then collapsed. The rat had fought, tearing with sharp teeth and claws but the sticky mass of its body separated and reformed. It absorbed the rat, digesting with strong acids oozed for this purpose the same acids that had blistered the kid's neck.

Warmth could always be found under the straw where bacteria fed and generated heat. The more heat the bacteria generated the more bacteria grew and the warmer It was. It understood light, heat and hunger. It also understood danger.

It never pondered its own existence although the farmer had pondered something very close to that when he had discovered its birthing. The farmer was not aware that one of his hens had spawned this thing, but he had found its green, leathery eggshell fragments the previous Christmas morning. The farmer thought that maybe a lizard egg had got in with the chicken eggs. Maybe it was just a rotten egg. The farmer was too simple to think on it for long and the whole matter was soon forgotten altogether.

It was smart enough to know that It needed to keep hidden. Aware of its own vulnerability, It was adept at keeping itself out of sight. It would find a way to survive this cold season although this was the leanest time It had experienced. It shifted its body, almost a shrug, and tried not to dwell on the fire that burned its skin. It was salivating and, like acid in an empty stomach that begins to dissolve the delicate lining, its own digestive fluids would feed on itself to stave off starvation. It had experienced times when more than half of its bulk had been lost this way. It beat dying. Spring would offer abundance for recuperation.

In the chicken coop below its favorite hiding spot in the loft, It heard the scratching and rustling of the birds. They scavenged for feed amongst the droppings and feathers on the floor and preened themselves of lice and fleas. It did not think of these creatures as food, they were the first thing It had known, and they had accepted it. They never made a fuss if It passed through their midst as though they knew that It held them in the same regard that a man holds his god. It would hide itself in the chicken shit, which offered perfect camouflage for its colouring and general texture. It moved in silence.

When It wandered outside to forage for food It could become so cold that movement was difficult. Under the setting hens It warmed itself, but It was vulnerable here since this was the area most often visited by the farmer and his family as they gathered eggs, tended their brood. It could feel the life growing inside the spotted, ivory shells and, in the closest thing that It could come to loneliness, considered a kinship with that life.

In the warm season, food was plenty, snakes, rats, spiders, grasshoppers, bats and occasional larger varmints. Foxes and raccoons sometimes made the mistake of looking for a meal in the barn and ended as one themselves. It preferred to enter its quarry through the mouth, feeding on the carcass from the inside. Soon all that remained would be a course powder of indigestible matter; barn dust.

Cautious of people who came to tend the animals, It would hide where It could watch them. Sometimes It would hang from a ceiling beam, mere inches above their head. It imagined tasting them; had considered consuming one. It always drew itself back, afraid. It knew they could communicate with each other. It was hungry enough right now to chance it, had started to with the kid. It ventured out in search of a safer meal.

It slid from its lair and down the ladder in a way a ladder was never meant to be used. Across the floor, folding upon itself, stretching and retracting, slithering and sometimes almost walking, It made its way among the rooster and hens. It squished through a narrow crack in the wall making the only sound It ever made; that of Jell-O forced between a child's missing teeth.

The air was stinging cold. It would soon become too stiff to be able to reshape itself.

It left no track in the snow. The ice crystals froze its edges solid. Stiff and cold, its edges were cut off if It crossed a sharp piece of ice. It felt no pain but knew It was losing pieces of itself. Had it not been for the burning hunger over its entire skin, It would have returned to the comfort of the nesting hens.

It made its way across a field and through a fence, just another shadow playing in the ripples on the snow. Bushes picked at It and tore off more small pieces. It meandered down a rabbit hole but was now too slow to catch the white snowshoe that escaped out the back door.

It knew that It had to find warmth soon or It would lose all ability to move. If It could have cursed the cold Canadian winter, It would have.

When It came out of the brush It sensed the dog even though it was just a black shape against the dark house behind it. This house sported no lights to invite Santa in. The dog smelled It and began to howl and pull at its tether chain.

It dragged itself across the snow-covered yard. It would be warm inside the dog. The pain would stop. Caution was forgotten as It advanced. It only considered the warmth and the food. It touched the dog's paw and tried to move faster but was unable. The warmth of the body acted like an aphrodisiac and more caution slipped. The dog lunged forward, jaws gaping to bite the intruder. The vicious snarl rumbling from the dog's throat turned to a yelp of pain when it bit down and found its mouth on fire. Lights came on in the house. A door slammed. A flashlight beam bounced along the ground.

Rob squinted through the darkness and tried to focus where his flashlight shone. "Rimjan. Damn dog. What's all the fuss boy?" Rob stepped closer to the animal, holding his housecoat closed with his free hand. The night air nipped at his bare legs. He shuffled forward a few more feet trying to see the dog, but it was squirming too fast for his alcohol bleared eyes to see well. He was beside it before he noticed that something was on the dog. Christ what was that? It was hard to see. Too curious to consider that it might be dangerous, Rob moved closer. Steam rose from the howling animal. What a racket. He moved to grab the dog's chain, to make it stand still so he could get a good look. The collar broke and the dog kicked like a bronco.

Unprepared for the animal's violent movements, It lost Its grip and flew in the air. When It landed It felt a body and sensed a change in texture. Hunger drove It toward the mouth It sensed a few inches away.

Flashlight trained on the animal as it kicked free and began rolling in the snow, Rob felt a weight strike his shoulder but was distracted by Rimjan's flaming red haunches and cries of pain. Dark stains streaked the snow where he had been rolling.

Rob turned to see what had grabbed his shoulder just before pain flared on his neck. Instinct made him grab at his neck. He felt a soft mass in his fingers. He couldn't hold it, his hands burned. He twisted around as he tried to throw It off. The burning intensified and he began to scream. He threw himself to the ground and rolled in the snow trying to put out the fire that was spreading toward his face.

It knew It had Its quarry good now. There was no way It was going to let go of this meal and the warmth that was promised. It couldn't make it back to the barn without warming up first; without feeding. It moved toward the mouth then realized what It was about to feed on. It had thought It was on the dog but now It knew it was one of the people. It paused, but there was no time for decision. It was too exposed; was too cold; too hungry. It was too late to stop. It pushed into the mouth, cutting off the screams. Rob's contortionist display continued as a thick acid burned his lips, tongue, nose, throat.

Judith saw her husband squirming on the ground and ran to him, her arms flailing. She skidded onto her knees and tried to still his movements. The way he clawed at his face and throat scared her. She thought he was choking but on what? He had come out to shut the dog up. Heart attack? Sure, that was it. The doctor had warned them that his heart was bad from all the drink and smoking. She stumbled toward the house to call for an ambulance. She didn't see the neighbors who had come out to investigate the commotion as they looked to her for explanation. She was intent on the phone and saving her husband.

It was warm and the pain of hunger was diminishing. Digestive acids had found soft tissue to work on. Oblivious to the commotion happening only inches away; It wallowed in the heat and the easing of Its own discomfort. It ignored warnings of Its instincts. As hunger abated and normal body temperature approached, It grew concerned over Its actions. It wasn't sure how to proceed.

The farmer's family had woken and investigated the continuous screams and yells of Rob and Judith. She had managed to call for an ambulance before succumbing to panic again. Another the farmer's wife added her own off pitch screeching. Her husband hit her once, but it did no good. Never did.

Flicking lights bounced off the buildings, out of place in this rural community that reflected the atmosphere of a western movie. The ambulance attendants were greeted by a small collection of figures in various forms of dress, none sporting the jackets and boots that the temperature called for. Ryan, a hunk of white gauze taped to the back of his neck, stood, smiling at the blazing, flashing lights of the ambulance, a magic Christmas display.

The medics grabbed their equipment and cleared a path through the people. No pulse, no breathing, pupils responding, mouth to mouth was started while other signs of injury were searched for. A quick pound to the chest produced a flutter. The heart was in defibrillation and shock would be necessary. All contact with Rob was removed a second before the paddles were discharged into him. The body heaved off the ground pushing against the paddles. Rob's chest caved in and the attendant found his hands fully inside of his patient.

Shock and surprise slowed reactions as the paramedic stared in horror at the hole he was up to his wrists in. Something black engulfed his hands and they started burning.

It was jolted like It never had been

before. Its body contracted in one massive convulsion. When It was next aware of itself, It was struck by the sudden cold. It tried to shake off the fog on Its senses and realized It was attached to a different human, and in the open.

A stir went through those gathered around Rob at what was hanging off one of the attendant's hands. At first it appeared to be part of Rob. When the screaming began and the thing dropped to the ground, the crowd scrambled out of its way. It moved with jumps and jerks and passed through the headlights of the ambulance. With a good look at It, they knew they had ever seen anything like it before.

Its forward movement halted often while It seemed to contemplate where It was going. It tried to move in several directions at once, would shake all over, then proceed again. It was almost out of the light before anyone moved.

"Holy ol' jumping", muttered Ryan's older brother. "Looks like the blob from the movie".

Ryan's mom ran away, his father ran toward the freakish creature, Ryan headed toward the garden shed in search of a weapons. This blob had to be dealt with the way oddities were dealt with in the country. Hunt it and kill it. Rob and the still screaming ambulance attendant were forgotten in light of this latest revelation. The game was on.

It knew It was in trouble. People were coming after It and It could hardly control itself. Convulsions racked its mass, sometimes pulling It into short periods of unconsciousness. Each time It awoke It was to a higher state of anxiety. It was getting cold. Its strength was being sapped by the muscle contractions. Not even sure whether It headed toward the barn or not, It simply moved away from the sound of the people.

Hooting and hollering, Ryan chased the darkness. Someone had enough sense to grab Rob's flashlight and now a beam of light cut through the dark, wavering off the trees and poking ahead like a futuristic sword waved by a cloaked figure.

It continued moving, the spasms easing but slowing It down, keeping It disoriented. Terror leading, It made Its way into as much darkness as It could. It knew the people were hampered by the darkness. It knew darkness only as a colder place. It would rather face cold than people. It continued moving.

It sensed heat through a thick curtain of branches. In a few minutes It found itself only feet away from the ambulance. It crawled underneath the idling vehicle and basked in the heat thrown down by the motor's fan. It slumbered for a few minutes but was roused by the change in pitch of the engine. The van started to move and It tried to dodge the approaching tire. Too late, the full weight of the truck pressed and jammed It down into the snow of the driveway.

Its flexible body was unhurt by the wheel but being flattened out thin caused much of Its mass to adhere to the snow beneath It and freeze. It would be slowed to a crawl if It tried to drag the frozen portion along. It would be sacrificing a lot of Its mass if It left the frozen portion behind. It could need that mass if feeding remained difficult. It decided to take as much of itself along as It could and began heading toward the barn. The dead weight of Its frozen self skidded behind It.

Soon It was almost to the barn. It could sense the warmth of the roosting pen where It could burrow beneath the sitting hens and warm Itself by the eggs of Its brethren. It stretched a little harder toward Its goal, more of Its mass was freezing, slowing It further.

"Aha, there you are" a light fell on it.

Ryan, full of the country, had kept vigil in the yard. He had set himself to guard the house. Now he had It in his sights. This would prove he was as tough as the rest of them. He swung the plastic snow shovel with his free hand and cut the thing on the ground in half. Part of It kept moving: a little faster now that It was free of some of the dead weight. Ryan took off after it.

"Trying to get the chickens eh? I'll lambaste you creep." The lack of fear proof of his innocence, Ryan placed himself between It and the barn. His young mind needed little coaxing to picture himself the hero of the day. He stood his ground and swung the shovel again, cutting through the snow inches in front of the thing. Ryan cursed his miscalculation and moved for another swing, but the thing veered, and his next attack was even further away. The blob changed course and headed into the scrap pile at the side of the barn. A tangle of roofing tin, fencing wire, boards and rusting machinery, Ryan knew he could not follow It, but he could make sure he got It when It came out. The pile was not so big that he couldn't watch it all. He set up siege. Even at the risk of not being in bed when Santa came, he remained on guard.

It was safe from the attack of the little person, but It knew It was again in big trouble. Most of It was gone and the rest was freezing up fast. Each time It tried to leave the pile where It hid, Ryan chased It back in. Slowly It became more and more difficult to move. It knew It would not see the inside of the barn again. It was going to freeze solid. Then what? It had no idea what Its body would do then. Would It die? Dissolve? Or would the spring thaw give It renewed life, like a frog hibernating in the mud. Its final thoughts were painless ones.

Ryan kept his vigil until the others returned from their fruitless hunt. He ran to them in his excitement but when he told the story of his adventure, he left out the part where he allowed part of it to escape into the scrap pile. He did not want them to think that he was just a runt who couldn't handle the situation. Besides, he reasoned, it had been more than an hour since he had seen It last so it must have been dead. He had cut It in half, what could survive that injury. He proudly showed the men the creature he had killed. He carried his trophy in the shovel that had been his sword in his battle. They praised his courage. Ryan raised a hand to the bandage on his neck thinking this was his best Christmas ever.

Spring came...

Footnote People In World History
by David Perlmutter

"Dude!"

Wendy caught me as I was trying to pry open the bottle of whiskey that I'd surreptitiously taken from the bar while everyone was partying, figuring that nobody would notice. I'd been sober most of that New Year's Eve, like I promised her earlier, but temptation was bound to get me, I suppose.

Look. If you're an attractive girl, it's hard enough going through life actually being ignored. And if you'd the unfortunate experience that I had just had, alcohol serves as a panacea. Maybe not the only or the best one, but still a good one. Anyway, there was Wendy, standing there in the doorway, with her checkerboard shirt and rakishly tilted faux-fur hat giving her the appearance of a hunter on the prowl. And I was her game.

"You told me that you'd given up the booze, Belle," she said.

"No, I didn't," I corrected her. "I said I wasn't drinking as much as I used to. I never said I was going to give it up entirely. Besides, the way things are, you need *something* to get through the days."

"Amen to that. Here; let me get that for you."

She went to the bottle, and opened it easily, as you'd expect the daughter of a northwestern lumberjack might be able to do. With glasses and ice from the mini-fridge, we started working on the bottle's contents.

We'd only met recently, but we'd bonded in friendship quickly. We had a lot of stuff in common. We were both daughters of extremely masculine men who expected a lot of us, but couldn't necessarily be there for us when we needed them to be. We were both in the late teens-early twenties age range, when girls become women seemingly overnight and are left to find their way through life without much of a biological road map. We'd both grown up without mothers to help us through trying times. We both had worked demanding and frustrating jobs for male bosses who didn't always get us (doubly troubling for me, since mine was also my dad). We both had a lot of male admirers, even very young ones. We both came from small towns where weird crap was always happening, and we'd learned pretty quickly how to be self-sufficient against most types of threats because of that. We both had red hair: mine being long and orange tinted, hers being short and the color of port wine.

And, as it turned out, we were both *really* the creations of people from other worlds, and thus didn't have complete control over our destinies. Which we were now trying to change by working independently, but with others, to get that control for ourselves.

I should probably explain that, even though I don't entirely get it myself.

You see, when an animated television program is created, a whole small universe is developed along with it. The creators of the programs spend a lot of time shaping how everything looks, acts, and feels, and that includes the people who live in the universe. However, they spent much more time and emphasis developing who the lead characters are, and all the supporting characters have to take what's left on the table after that to figure out who they are. And when a show ends, and a universe basically gets rubbed out of existence, you have a lot of people who are out of not just a job, but a whole way of life.

Bad enough trying to be a lead character living without a full existence, but what about if you're *just* a supporting character?

Which was what I was told, condescendingly, when they shut down my universe and life.

The worst part about that was, up until then, I thought I was living a "normal" life in the "real" world. And then to discover otherwise! To say I was shocked, devastated and angry, among other things, would be the mildest of understatements.

That was another thing Wendy and I had bonded over. She'd been "duped" the same way. But, unlike me, she was used to dealing with fakes and frauds. Her old workplace was full of them, headed by her boss. So she could smell them a mile away, whereas I was a lot greener. The advice she'd given me about that had come in handy.

As it turned out, we were far from the only ones who had been "duped". Television animation shows tend to have a short shelf life, and so universes are capriciously created and destroyed at whim, with nary a thought to what might become of the creatures inhabiting them after the ax falls. Because we were not "real" people, with off-stage lives, property, votes and dependents, the theory went, we could be treated as if we did not really "exist", and be used and abused in all senses of the word.

Those of us who had been exiled from our "homes" did not take kindly to this idea. With the idea of taking back what was "rightfully ours", we were now actively pursuing any sort of activity we could to get our point across. From social media campaigns, to class-action lawsuits against the big studios that had "created" us, to acts of "terrorism" (at least according to the government, because we've really gotten on their bad side). This was all under the banner of the Cartoon Republican Army, of which Wendy and I had become members as soon as we could. We were proudly, at that time, wearing our regulation armbands (which, unfortunately, look like the ones the Nazis used to wear on their uniforms, only with the group initials in place of the infamous swastika).

That was the whole reason we were where we were in the first place. An isolated hotel, up on a perilous set of stone cliffs, with only a small seaport as the nearest human contact. Was there a better place to spend what would have been an otherwise lonely as hell holiday season for the vast majority of us "toons"? The CRA leadership thought so, and they proceeded to buy up a huge number of the available rooms at the place. The management was delighted, because they don't get nearly that many visitors most of the time, and we were putting a lot of the mean greens in their pocket doing that.
But they didn't stay delighted. Not by a long shot.

* * *

The evening had started out reasonably enough, with a discussion of how our joint identities and goals bonded us, and an attempt to figure out where we wanted to go from there. That didn't last. Sure enough, as I kind of thought they would, those who were more interested in partying than politics had high-jacked the whole affair. They got the booze out, some of which had been brought there, and some of it the hotel's personal stash. Now here it was NYE, and a fair number of us had been sloppy drunk for a long time before then. You could tell by all the inebriated bodies tossed around the floors. Though some of them weren't inebriated enough to make grabs at my tits and ass. Even when I swore and kicked and threw punches at them, they wouldn't let up. I was lucky to get back to the room with my whiskey and virginity still intact.

It might have been all right if we had stuck to what we brought and not drunk up the hotel's resources. Including all of the concierge's beloved Sam Adams. This would undoubtedly be the first and only time we'd been staying at this place, if he had his way.

When I finished my first glass of whiskey, I went to the window, and longingly gazed out of it, over the long high cliffs, pass the seaport, and onto the long and unforgiving expanse of the Atlantic Ocean. Then I turned to Wendy and, quoting Peggy Lee, said:

"Is that all there is?"

"All there is to what?" Wendy asked.

"You know. Life. Specifically, *our* lives. Or, at least, the ones we *used* to have."

"How so?"

"You know what I mean. Supporting characters in other people's lives. Not being able to be fully grown, fully dimensional, independent people. What kind of life is that to live?"

"We were only "supporting" characters because the narratives of the shows chose to define us *as* "supporting characters," Wendy reminded me. "In our own minds, on our own terms, in our own lives, especially in the parts that the camera didn't see, we were leads."

"You mean, like when we went to the bathroom...."

"*Besides* that. When we were working and stuff."

"Neither of us had jobs that were really exciting."

"Which was probably why we were supporting characters, and not leads."

"But why create us at all? I always had the sneaking suspicion that the producers of my show created me just to be eye candy, and nothing else. I mean, just as I was coming up the staircases in the lobby to get to the elevator, there were a few drunk guys getting fresh. Like "MeToo in embryo.""

"Our guys, or locals?"

"Who do you think? You know how scared most of the hotel staff is of us."

"Why? Is it that B.S. about us being capricious gods and goddesses willing and able to kill if and when we want to? I don't trust the media to get anything right about us, just like they can't get it right about anything or anybody else anymore. Besides, the only things those kind of guys need, regardless of race, is to have their balls kicked up into their pelvises. That's what I did when they tried it with me when I followed you up here."

Suddenly, we heard knocking on the door, and slurred voices. I knew it was the fellows who had tried stuff with me earlier. How had they found out where I was?

I flushed and tried to escape to the room, but Wendy motioned me back to the bed I was sitting on.

"Never mind about them," she said. "I'll deal with them."

And, bravely, she undid the chain lock on the hotel door and stepped outside. There was a flurry of swearing, and the sounds of tautly thrown punches and kicks, and then fast footsteps in retreat. Then Wendy returned, her clothes unruffled and her hair hardly out of place.

"You dealt with them," I said, admirably.

"Yeah," she answered. "A lot of the dumber boys don't think a girl would ever have the courage to attack them. So, when they do, it's kind of unknown territory, and they're the ones who suddenly can't deal with it. Not like us."

"I'll remember that," I responded. "But what do we do now?"

"As in what? Work?"

"Mostly."

"We're more fortunate than most of that crew downstairs, because we have actual real-world job experience that we can translate into jobs here in the "real" world. There's always going to be a restaurant in need of a waitress, given the turnover rate, so you shouldn't have trouble. As for me, the amount of time I spent being bored behind a counter before is probably going to lead to me being bored behind another one sooner or later, if my C.V. is taken seriously."

"But what if, you know, we end up having a new boss who....tries to take advantage...."

"They wouldn't *dare*." Wendy was adamant on this point. "Not in this day and age. I just showed you the folly of that, didn't I? And besides: social media sucks in a lot of ways, but it can be a brilliant way of taking down an unjust attacker if it's used the right way. And, besides, if other human men are as....well...beguiled.....by us as the men working here are, they're doubly as likely to want to make trouble. All that **B.S.** about all us 'toon girls being man-eating, ball-breaking vampires was good for scaring them off of us, at least."

Then we heard what sounded like a gunshot, which startled me.

"What was that?" I said. "You don't think that was one of us....with a gun....?"

"That was a flare," said Wendy. "Not a bullet. Trust me- I know the difference." She looked at her watch. "It's 11:59 now. Somebody probably just decided to launch the New Year early. I think I need another shot. What about you?"

I nodded. And we proceeded to do that, as everyone else counted down from 10 to 1 as best they could, and welcomed the New Year in as the two of us did.

With a strong sense of faith who we were, but with a still strong and lingering sense of fear of the unknown world and life ahead of us.

A Visit for Mithras
by Daniel Fisher

'Twas the night before Mithras, and all through my house
The only bitches stirring were me and my irritating spouse;
Herbs were drying on the great hearth with only the mildest of care,
In hopes the great bulls dying would bring prosperity here;
My nag wanted me to snuggle in bed, but with his odor, I didn't dare;
Visions of sexy time danced in his head, I'd rather work through the night; then even attempt a dare.
Perfumed in Axe spray, and I searching for my inhaler, this relationship was doomed if forced to nap there,
I just settled my brain on the next big chapter, writing furiously before I headed to the crapper,
When outside my window I heard some glass shatter,
Annoyed by the noise I leered out the window to see what was the matter.
Away to the window I dragged my fat ass,
Glared through the shutters and pulled up the sash.
The moon on this night showed off the slush in the glow,
Grey and sickly dirty snow just below,
Angry that people suck, what to my eyes did appear,

But a minivan and some dude holding cheap
   crappy beer,
This ugly ass driver so drunk and so quirky,
I knew from the red hat he was all **MAGA** and
   kind of jerky.
Bitching and moaning and whining a ton,
Bellowing and shouting, and using derogatory
   terms best used by none:
"Now, expletives and oh, that was lame. I dare not
   repeat some of those names!"
Stumbling to the top of the porch! Looking like
   he'd fall!
Now sashay away you cray - cray freak before we
   start to brawl
As leaves that before they crumple and die,
This drunken fool missed a step or two and I
   wished he would cry.
Up on my porch now, what's this idiot gonna do?
With fowl words he used cursing something about
   Jews, I headed down to meet this dink,
And then, a pounding, I heard at my door so I
   dared not to blink
The scratching and prying of a misfit key in the
   lock.
As I drew up my glock, watching for a sign,
This dumbass shoves through the door breaking
   the front, my lock now broken, why was he so
   thick?
Clearly not his house, he was dressed all in denims,

his shirt covered in what I hoped was his drink,
His clothes were all brandished in confederate
flags; and food stains I think....?
Broken bottles all over my porch, oh Hel no I said!
Had this been planned I'd have used the ritual
dagger in a blink,
That would be a great joy as he simply stood
scratching his sack.
His eyes—how glazed over they were, his face as
red as a cherry!
His nose like cauliflower, veiny and the hair was so
scary!
Drool spilling out of his mouth, slobbering on the
bottle dangling below,
And the beard on his chin had Cheetos in I just
know;
A joint hanging out the side of his lips was still lit
between his teeth,
And the smoke, reeking of cheap weed, bad
enough he broke in my place, now I got
skunkweed smell in my face;
The madder I became by this intruder with his
nasty face and a stammering pace.
He was making me sick just looking at the sight; if
not for being pissed I'd have puked on him this
night.
He was crabby and chapped, lips and face, like
roadkill in so many ways,
I cocked my gun and leveled to his face, I'd give

this bastard a chance to flee my space;
A nod of the head and drooping of his eyes
   showed he had no way to surmise
Oh well he was too fucked up to be surprised;
I clicked my glock pulling the trigger,
My bullet hit his face he turned with a jerk,
It being 2020 no one would question some dick
   dead on the ground,
Giving a nod I reached for the phone, the popo
   would soon come around;
He laid still as gust of cold wind blew my ways,
And I silently gave thanks on this most holy of
   days.
The bull is dead and I live in a stand your ground
   state.
*"Happy Mithras my dears drink your blood before
   it gets too late."*

Shadow

Have you ever had the feeling that you were being drawn towards something important, but weren't exactly certain what you were supposed to do until you got there?

You felt like you were made of metal, a huge magnet was pulling you along, making certain you told your story.

Making certain you were in the right place.

It all started when, as sort of a Christmas present to ourselves, my wife and I bought a new house.

My stress level skyrocketed.

You know, the whole new home thing.

Packing, meeting with bankers, house closings, moving out, moving in, all that stuff.

According to statistics, moving is the third most stressful event in most people's lives. Right behind marriage and divorce.

They say divorce is more stressful than marriage. Whoever compiled that report never met my wife. Ha! Ha!

We moved into the new house the weekend before Thanksgiving.

I started feeling sick right about that same time.

I felt some unusual pain, had some breathing difficulties and was even urinating blood.

I didn't worry about it. I figured stress was causing all my physical problems.

That, and maybe some strain from lifting too many heavy boxes.

Whatever the reason, I couldn't let it stop me. There were too many things to do.

So, I kept on going. Just like the Energizer Bunny!

I returned to work on Monday morning after moving furniture, boxes, and tons of other stuff all weekend.

I went in to do my job despite the pain and the difficulty I was having catching my breath.

After all, people had been telling me for years that stress can cause all kinds of physical problems.

I figured that stress was causing me to be sick and it would go away when the unpacking was done. Plus, I needed the money. We had just moved into a new house.

I kept working.

By Tuesday the pain had gotten so bad, I decided to leave work early and drive myself to the emergency room.

I drove myself because I didn't want to be an inconvenience by asking someone to take me to the ER, and I sure wasn't going to spring for the cost of an ambulance!

Not just for some stress-related illnesses.

I figured the doctors would run some tests and give me something for the stress.

Problem solved!

When I arrived at the hospital, the ER was pretty crowded, so I figured the process was going to take longer than I originally thought.

I was in for a nice surprise!

Shortly after I checked in, a nurse came into the waiting room, helped me into a wheelchair, and took me to an examination room!

She told me that since my breathing was labored and I was suffering from chest pains, hospital policy dictated that I had to be taken to an examination room immediately.

I went straight to the head of the line.

The examination room was small, but it had a bed, some monitors, and a sink.

The ER nurse asked me to take my clothes off and put on a hospital gown.

You know, one of those things that are open in the back so your butt is hanging out all the time.

The nurse said as soon as I get changed, I should lie down on the bed.

Then a different nurse came into my room, poked a needle in my arm, and took blood samples.

She inserted an IV tube in one of the veins in my arm and taped it down. She said she was leaving an IV in my arm as a precaution in case they needed to take more blood or give me medication.

I told her I was old enough to swallow pills.

She laughed, told me to try to relax, and left the room.

Before I could get settled, the first nurse came rushing back into my room, pushing a cart with a weird machine on it. She told me to lie back and relax. Then she started pasting little stickers on my chest.

You know the kind I'm talking about. They're like big postage stamps with metal buttons on one side and super stickum on the other.

The stickers are always so cold they feel like they'd been stored in a refrigerator.

When the nurse had the stickers pasted all over my chest, she started to clip wires to the metal buttons.

The wires ran from the buttons to a machine she had wheeled into my little room earlier.

All those wires were making me a little nervous, so I asked the nurse what she was doing.

She was very nice! She could tell I was a little frightened, so she patiently explained the machine to me.

She told me the machine she was hooking me up to is called an EKG. She said EKG stands for electrocardiogram. It was going to measure the electrical impulses of my heart. Those electrical impulses, she said, are transferred over the wires attached to my chest to the EKG, where they are printed out for medical professionals to interpret.

The printout looks a lot like the squiggly lines from a lie detector.

As soon as the machine stopped running, the nurse ripped the paper off the printer and glanced at it. She said it looked good to her, but she still needed to show it to the doctor for final approval.

She bustled out of the room still clutching the printout in her hand.

Since I was already in bed, I took a little nap.

Before I knew it, a doctor popped in to see me.

He told me his name was Doctor Wang. He said he was the resident ER physician.

Doctor Wang said he had read my EKG and it was normal.

In other words, I wasn't having a heart

attack. That news helped me relax a little more.

Doctor Wang had me sit up in bed so he could listen to my lungs with his stethoscope.

He told me to breathe normally.

While I was breathing, Doctor Wang placed the stethoscope on different spots along my back and my chest. He listened carefully so he could hear my lungs clearly.

After just a few minutes, the doctor put the stethoscope in his pocket and looked at me with a slight frown on his face.

He told me my lungs didn't sound quite right.

He said my lungs might be the reason for my chest pains, but the blood in my urine was an additional troubling symptom, completely unrelated to my lungs.

He suggested I have a CT scan to sort things out.

Since he was the doctor, I agreed.

The CT scan was performed in the radiology department next to where they do the X-rays.

In the CT room, a technician had me lie down on a moving cot that slid inside a small round tube where the CT scan takes place.

It was quick and easy. I was back in the ER in less than an hour.

Doctor Wang showed up in my room

before I even got back in bed.

I began to suspect that something was wrong.

Doctor Wang's frown was a little deeper.

He informed me the CT scan showed that I had pneumonia.

He said it also showed that I had an unusually enlarged gallbladder.

He said he believed the gallbladder was dangerously infected and needed to be removed.

I told him I had become kind of attached to my gallbladder and would prefer keeping it.

Doctor Wang didn't laugh at my joke, but he did smile slightly. He said he understood.

Then he told me he had already contacted a specialist about my gallbladder.

He said the specialist was on his way to the ER to consult on my case.

Doctor Wang suggested we didn't get upset about the possibility of losing the gallbladder until after we heard what the specialist had to say.

Doctor Wang washed his hands at the sink and quietly left the examination room.

I wasn't sure why Doctor Wang said "we" shouldn't worry. I was the one with the defective gallbladder.

Since he was the doctor and knew about these things, I decided to take another nap.

I woke to the sound of strange voices.
The gallbladder specialist and Doctor
Wang were in my room talking to me. They
were talking even before I was completely awake!

Do you know how hard it is to wake up
from a really good nap?

That's how I was feeling when the
specialist introduced himself.

I was still half asleep and could only
understand part of what the doctors were saying.

For instance, I forgot the specialist's name
as soon as he said it.

From then on, I just called him Doctor
G.

You know, G for gallbladder!

Doctor G told me he had reviewed my
CT scan, and conferred with Doctor Wang
about my case.

Doctor G told me my gallbladder was
"compromised," and should be removed.

However, the CT scan and my earlier
blood tests indicated a severe infection in my
gallbladder and lungs.

Doctor G said the infection was so bad,
immediate surgery would be risky.

He recommended a simple, routine
procedure designed to help get the infection
under control. The procedure involved inserting
a tube into my gallbladder to drain off the

infected fluids.

The procedure would be followed by an intense round of antibiotics.

Doctor G told me he could schedule the procedure for the following day.

He said I would need to stay overnight so I could be prepared for the procedure in the morning.

The procedure was so simple, Doctor G said, most people who have it done go home a few hours after the tube is inserted.

Since he was the doctor, I agreed to the procedure.

My wife was at the new house unpacking boxes. I called her to let her know what was happening.

Since it was going to be a routine procedure, she said she wanted to finish some things at the house and would come to the hospital later.

I was transferred to a room on the surgical prep wing.

My wife showed up to visit for a couple hours in my new hospital room. We talked about what was going to happen the next day and decided she should go to work in the morning.

After all, the procedure was routine, and we needed the money. We had just moved into a new house!

I went right to sleep after she left. I had nothing to worry about.

Early the next morning, a small group of doctors marched into my room. I had never met most of them, but Doctor G bought up the rear and I relaxed.

Doctor G said they had come to explain my upcoming procedure. To tell me more about the simple and safe procedure designed to eliminate poisons from my system.

Doctor G said the procedure would begin with a small incision in my side. He told me that a surgeon would be performing the incision at the beginning of the procedure, but the bulk of the task would be performed by a robot controlled by technicians.

Doctor G was very excited about the robot. He said it has never failed.

Doctor G said I wouldn't even need a general anesthetic.

He told me a nurse would inject me with a local anesthetic that would prevent me from feeling any pain at the incision site.

The surgeon performing the incision would test the area to make certain I could feel no pain before he made any cuts.

As soon as the incision was safely completed, the technicians Doctor G had mentioned earlier would insert a small tube into my stomach cavity via the opening the surgeon in charge of the procedure had just made. Doctor G said the technicians would be using a robot as their surgical tool.

Using the robot and its internal cameras, the technicians would snake the tube through my stomach until reaching my gallbladder. They would also be using the robot's cameras to track what was happening inside me.

A small needle in the hose's end was designed to pierce the infected gallbladder and insert a drain tube. The puncture would be sealed off and the infected fluids building up in my gallbladder would empty through the tube into a collection bag that would hang loosely from my right side.

Once the infections were under control, Doctor G said, surgeons would be able to safely remove my gallbladder. The doctors all agreed that the entire process should be completed in about two weeks.

The infection would be under control, my lungs would be cleared, my gallbladder would be removed, and I would be on my way to recovery.

Easy, peasy! I was looking forward to seeing the robot and getting the whole thing over with.

Doctor G emphasized the simplicity of the procedure and the success rate of the robotic team. He asked me to sign a paper giving my permission for the procedure before he left the room to complete his rounds.

Since he was the doctor, I signed the form.

Several hours later, a nurse came to my room to tell me my surgery was scheduled for early in the afternoon.

The crack team of robotic experts known lovingly as "The Geek Squad" would not be available until then.

The nurse optimistically informed me the procedure was routine, and I should be released early Friday morning.

Usually, the nurse added, patients return in two to four weeks to have the hose and gallbladder removed.

I called my wife to tell her the newest developments.

She said she would come straight to the hospital from work.

Since I was already in bed, I took a nap.

Later that afternoon, I was wheeled down to the first-floor surgical annex where a group of four computer technicians, a member of the anesthesiologist team, and Doctor G, waited impatiently for me to arrive.

I was quickly transferred to an operating table surrounded by computers and monitors. I was told to relax.

Everything will be just fine, Doctor G said.

The procedure began just as Doctor G had described it that morning.

A nurse administered a few relatively painless injections of a local anesthetic.

Just a little pinprick.

Doctor G made sure I couldn't feel anything by poking me a couple of times before he made his incision.

Four technicians were hovering nearby waiting for Doctor G to complete his tasks.

This was the "Geek Squad."

They were gathered around two computer terminals at a safe distance from the surgeon.

They were careful not to cause any distractions.

Distractions can cost time and they knew they were only one patient away from the long holiday weekend.

Once Doctor G was satisfied with his work, he moved back a few steps to allow room for two of the technicians to position the surgical robot next to my side.

The robot looked like a large cable TV box. It was rectangular, with a bunch of wires and tubes that seemed to sprout from one side.

The other side had several vertical vents running from the top of the box to its bottom.

It was mounted longwise on a wheeled cart with adjustable legs.

Using medical tape and straps, the technicians attached the robot directly over my side with the tubes and wires facing the incision.

The robot's wires were hooked up to matching wires coming from a large server style computer located at the foot of the operating table.

Guided by the technicians at the computer monitors, a miniature robotic arm with a small drain tube encircling it entered my stomach through the incision in my side.

I didn't feel a thing. The only reason I knew what was happening was because I was awake and the technicians were reporting their progress to the surgeon.

The other two technicians remained close to the computer terminals where they kept a close watch on the progress of the robotic arm.

These technicians were assigned the task of monitoring the drain tube via cameras as it entered my stomach. Once the tube reached my gallbladder, they were responsible for making certain the needle was inserted and the tube was properly connected.

Doctor G left the room as soon as the

drain tube was inserted into the incision. The nurse anesthesiologist followed quickly behind, leaving me in the hands of the operating room technicians.

The technicians worked quickly. This was, after all, a routine procedure.

So routine in fact, as they followed the drain tube's progress through my stomach cavity, the technicians began a loud, animated discussion about their holiday weekend plans.

In the style of the old M.A.S.H. television series, the technicians competed to see which one could come up with the most inebriated, revolting plan for his time off.

I thought the banter was amusing and even suggested a few establishments that might meet their desires. I was blatantly ignored.

The procedure was completed in record time.

The team of technicians were in a rush to begin their weekend.

One of the technicians called the fifth floor to arrange for an orderly to come pick me up, while the other technicians rapidly removed the robotic attachments and performed a basic clean-up of the area.

The fifth-floor staff informed the technicians that all the orderlies remaining on duty were tied up, so there was going to be a delay before someone was sent to get me.

The technicians weren't willing to wait.

It was quickly decided that the technician with the least amount of time in the job, the same one who was tasked with calling the fifth-floor staff, would be responsible for getting me back to my room.

As soon as the decision was made, the team of technicians gathered around and carefully moved me from the operating table to a gurney. After I was comfortably situated on the gurney, three of the technicians hurried out of the room, leaving me behind with the new guy.

The technician assigned with the task of seeing me back to my room was kind and soliciting, but he was also in a hurry to get his weekend started.

He covered me with a blanket and rolled my gurney out the door of the operating room and into the adjoining hallway.

The hallway was dark and deserted.

The hospital personnel assigned to the x-ray wing of the hospital had all left work early to begin their holiday weekend.

No one was in the offices.

I felt out of sorts when we exited the surgery and entered the abandoned hallway. Something didn't feel right, but I couldn't quite put my finger on what was bothering me.

At first, I passed the feeling off as the effect of being in an empty hospital, but the feeling grew stronger as we passed the closed examination room doors, and darkened, empty offices.

The technician was talking non-stop as he pushed my gurney down the center of the abandoned corridor. The hallway was long and eerily quiet, and his voice began to echo in my head.

I spotted something out of the corner of my eye as we passed one of the rooms. I quickly looked that way to see what it was, but we were moving too fast.

I only saw a shadow.

I figured the dim lights of the hallway were just playing tricks with my eyes.

I was a little spooked.

I concentrated on the next doorway, watching it closely as we approached.

I didn't see anything unusual until we drew parallel with the opening.

There, in the doorway, was a silhouette of a human being. I could see the shape of its head and shoulders. I pushed myself slightly up on the gurney to get a better look and was able to make out the darkened shape of a woman's body on the door.

I gasped in fear.

Silhouettes appeared in each doorway we passed.

Darkened shapes of men and women, all of them seeming to stare directly at me!

Then I noticed the silhouettes began to move out of the doorways and follow my gurney!

I took a deep breath and laid back on the gurney.

I asked the technician pushing me what the silhouettes were.

He slowed down and looked over his shoulder.

He said he didn't see anything.

He rolled the gurney into the main hallway and started talking again.

The silhouettes disappeared as we rolled under the bright lights of the main hallway and onto an elevator.

I breathed a sigh of relief and began to relax.

My hospital room was a short distance from the elevator. I would soon be able to sleep.

I figured the silhouettes were just another symptom of my stress.

But when the elevator doors opened on the fifth floor, there were silhouettes everywhere.

They crowded the hallway and hovered in every doorway.

I thought they were going to stop us from

getting to my room, but the silhouettes blocking the hallway parted silently to allow us to pass.

Five feet away from my room, the technician rolling the gurney came to a stop.

He said it would be good for me to walk the remaining few steps to my bed.

I think he had finally seen, or possibly sensed, the hallway full of dark silhouettes.

He turned and moved rapidly towards the elevator.

The silhouettes in the hallway had formed a half-circle around me. They were all looking directly at me. A few were even beginning to reach out, to almost touch me!

I turned to face my room, hoping for a means of escape, but what I saw made the terror even worse.

Laying on my hospital bed was a clearly defined, dark black silhouette.

The silhouette's head and shoulders moved as he turned to face me.

He looked as if he were alive.

Even the shape of his body and legs were clearly outlined. He moved just like me!

I cried out in terror as I attempted to get up from my gurney and run!

One of the floor nurses heard me. She quickly stepped away from the patient in the neighboring room and rushed to my side to help me.

Before the nurse could reach my gurney, I had managed to sit up.

With the terror of the silhouette in my mind, I quickly slid off the gurney and took a hesitant step towards the elevator. The nurse believed I was just disoriented and headed in the wrong direction.

She took hold of my left arm and gently turned me back towards my room.

The darkened figure had risen from my bed and stood in the doorway.

I looked up and down the corridor, hoping to find a means of escape. Instead, hundreds more silhouettes had appeared. Some were standing in doorways; some were loitering in the hallway.

Every one of them looked directly at me.

My chest suddenly felt heavy, my breathing became labored, and my heart rate started to climb.

The nurse helping me to my room noticed my shallow breathing and loudly requested assistance.

She was immediately joined by a second nurse who took hold of my right arm.

The two nurses were all that kept me from falling to the floor.

Both nurses told me to take deep

breathes and remain calm.

I tried to tell them about the silhouettes, that I couldn't take deep breathes because of my fear, but the words wouldn't come.

Gasping for air, I looked around once more for help.

I saw the silhouette who had been laying in my bed.

He was slowly making his way towards me, his arms extended towards me like the shadow of an old zombie ghost.

The corridor had become full of silhouettes.

Darkened outlines of men, women, even children were closing in around me.

My chest became heavier, my breathing and heart rate spiked. I began having seizures.

The head nurse had come from out of nowhere to inject me with 100 mg of phenobarbital in an attempt to stop the seizures.

She informed her co-workers that she had already summoned the crash cart and its crew.

The silhouette drew closer. My heart raced with fear, my breathing was completely out of control.

My seizures had reached a grand mal stage.

I was injected with another 100 mg of

phenobarbital.

The silhouette had reached my side. He reached out and took my hand.

He had been waiting in my room for me to arrive. All the silhouettes had been waiting expectantly for me.

The silhouette tugged gently on my hand, and a second silhouette, so light in color that it was almost transparent, was slowly pulled from my body.

One nurse announced that my heart rate was above 200 beats per minute. Another nurse cried out that the crash cart had arrived.

I looked at the new silhouette standing beside me and realized my time had come. The routine procedure had failed.

The poisons the tube was supposed to drain were coursing through my system.

My heart stopped beating.

The two silhouettes merged, creating a lighter, stronger Shadow.

For a brief moment, I stood over my body watching the brave nursing staff as they took courageous measures to bring me back, but it was too late.

I am now just the essence of who I once was.

I know you can't hear me.

Even if you could, you wouldn't

understand why I was telling you all this.

Yet.

I was drawn to this operating room, to stand outside.

Patiently waiting.

You are inside the operating room, having your own routine procedure performed.

I am just a silhouette in a doorway.

You'll be meeting me soon.

Merry Christmas!

The Fourth Grave of Marisa Enver Blyth...

by Sergio 'PALUMBO

There were a number of different styles of graves in cemeteries, the same as cemetery statues and sculptures, and the 26-year-old woman, despite her age, could say she knew many of them. Those, certainly, reflected the diversity of cultural practices around death and how it changed over time. Early urban cemeteries were churchyards, but she had never visited any of them, at least not so far. Not surprisingly, it had also been said that graves were associated with paranormal activity with many locals claiming to have seen apparitions moving through the tightly compacted tombstones, with even a strange ghostly shadow walking around occasionally. Well, she didn't know about that, and that was not the reason why she was here today.

Because it was that time of vacation for her during the year again, and the woman had come to pay her respects to the dead, just the day before Halloween, as she was used to do...

That small cemetery situated near that village was a publicly accessible space but with private graves. Wrapped in her dark overcoat, she walked the stone path leading from the boundary trees to the area where most of the tombs were located. There a few statues added on the top of some graves, but in most cases you could easily see around the headstones that looked like dirty marble objects spurting out of the ground. Nobody else happened to be around, seemingly, and she knew that people rarely came here. After all, the village nearby was very tiny and its population was made up of very old citizens. Children were hardly ever spotted in the small grid of local streets, but they occasionally showed up with their parents when they paid a visit to their grandparents.

Most people undoubtedly did not want to be alone in this place, but the case of this woman was different. She had to come here alone, of course, but in a way she couldn't say she was really alone, at the same time... Her name was Marisa Enver Blyth and, like everyone else, she was not a frequent visitor of this burial ground. As her eyes finally spotted the grave she was looking for - with that old small garden statue of her home she well knew as she herself had put it there...- a sensation of sadness and dejection had the better of her. Things were always like that when she was near that tomb, anyway.

The young woman considered that the purpose of cemeteries like this could surely extend beyond the community's need for burial space. The reasons for having a cemetery changed over time, and included issues over public health and a desire to offer protection and privacy, both to the corpses and to the bereaved.

It was also a way of demonstrating a degree of civic pride, at least until the locals living nearby became too old to take care of the cemetery and the people buried within started being forgotten.

Of course, this wasn't the case with Marisa Enver Blyth herself. The woman scratched at her short chestnut curls and whispered something. She knew perfectly well where the gravestone she was searching for stood and had her own reasons to keep visiting this place from time to time. So many stories had been told about cemeteries but none of them were similar to the woman's reason, at least as far as she knew.

As her steps approached the small statue and the tomb and stopped before it, a thought crossed the woman's mind. **'I sometimes happen to visit my own grave...'**, she told herself. As she was thinking about that, her dark eyes stared at the name that was written on the marble of the headstone, which read: **'Marisa Enver Blyth, born 1st November 2048 - deceased 31th October 2071.'** No other biographical data was on the marker.

Curious, you might say. The name of the dead woman buried in that grave was the same of the one who had come to visit it today, and, *even stranger than that*, she had died just three years before her, although the photo of the deceased woman on the stone didn't differ too much from the present appearance of the visitor herself. Actually, this wasn't just a coincidence, there was more to it than met the eye...

As the woman stepped on the ground around the tomb, putting hers left hand on it, other recollections took over her mind.

Fission was the right word to indicate what had happened. Though, the woman didn't precisely know how it occurred. What other term might she make use of to explain that, after all? Marisa wasn't a scientist when she first experienced it, but she had done much investigating since then, intensely studying that part of biology, trying to figure out what might be the cause of it all. Well, not that she had made sense of the whole thing, at least not yet.

The young woman had always been told, since she was a child, and she was still a believer, that a human soul separated from the body of the deceased once they passed away, to go up to Heaven, or to Hell - if you just reputed those things to be real of course. Well, what she had never imagined might happen was that the body of the deceased one himself might also separate from the corpse, in order to allow a copy of his, or of hers, to spring to life again, while the dead remains were put underground. Just like the one she stood before now.

Fission, in science, was the division of a

single living being into two or more parts and the regeneration of those parts into separate organisms resembling the original. The objects experiencing fission were usually cells, but the term might also be used to indicate the process experienced by some populations, or species, which divided into discrete parts. The fission could be binary fission, in which a single living being produced two parts, or multiple fission, in which a single one produced multiple parts.

In Marisa's case, every time she died, a separate individual came to life, as old as the deceased one, while her previous body simply dropped to the ground, dead. And she didn't know what happened to the soul, but she had ceased being a true believer long ago, after everything that she had undergone, as you could easily understand.

And it had happened to her four times so far...

After going through that difficult experience the first time, and on each occasion after that, the woman had tried to comprehend what had occurred, but her knowledge about science hadn't helped her much. After all, she had been a young professional driver in those days and certainly not an academician of any sort.

During the following months, she had

studied the whole thing in depth. As the years went by, she had tried to discover the secret of her body-fission though what she discovered hadn't proved helpful.

Organisms like Archaea and Bacteria reproduced with binary fission, which was known and easily explained in texts. It was known that binary fission resulted in the reproduction of living cells by dividing the cells themselves into two parts, each with the potential to grow to the size of the original. But this also meant that such process was used by some smaller, simpler living beings on Earth, and certainly not by large animals, nor by mammals like humans of course.

So, what had really happened to her?

Marisa hadn't been very smart the first time it had occurred, so she had simply run as fast as she could, away from the site where she had left her previous dead body. As a matter of fact, it was only during the second time, three years after the first fission, that the young woman had been able to take some samples of her deceased copy - hair and cells mostly - so she could have something just at her disposal to study, trying to explain what continued to happen to her.

She was sorry to say that she hadn't been able to find out the reason this kept happening, nor a way to prevent it from occurring again, through the following years.

What Marisa knew for certain, was that her DNA seemed capable of attaching each copy to a different part of the cell membrane in her next himself. The consequence of that asexual, and unprecedented to humans, method of reproduction was that all the cells were genetically identical, meaning that they had the same genetic material. No mutations ever occurred, according to the samples he had taken from her previous dead copies.

Marisa had undergone that frightening experience four times by now, and every single time she had had to run, as the young woman knew that she couldn't explain to the police how a copy of her present body lay lifeless on the ground while she was still walking around. There was no record of her having an identical brother, of course, and there was no way for her to explain how this was possible... Also she was afraid that she might be taken into custody, or treated as a subject to be studied in some secret labs, unbeknownst to the rest of Mankind. She imagined that during those tests she might be forced to suffer for who knows how long, too.

This certainly wasn't how Marisa wanted to live her life, and this was also why she had paid, every single time, a different scientist to examine the samples she brought to them. But the conclusions had always been unclear, as those men of science had told her that, undoubtedly, some further studies needed to be made, and that many more expensive tests were certainly necessary, in the presence of the authorities.

It was at those words that she, every single time, preferred to give up and walk away. The woman didn't want to be taken by the authorities to become a prisoner, subject to painful field studies that she would regret having started. She believed it would be unsafe to have confidence in academicians that she didn't know, or who could easily sacrifice her freedom for their disreputable purposes.

For a long time, Marisa had been uncertain about how this might be possible and, most of all, why it had happened to her. Maybe it was all connected to a vacation she had taken many years ago, when she had stayed at a resort in Russia near a small lake. The locals had told her that those waters were not a good place to swim, not anymore, though she didn't comprehend exactly what they said. Regretfully, she didn't speak the language very well... Or maybe it was because of something else altogether, a substance that had been released from the industries into those deeps. Anyway, the woman would never know now, as that area had soon become involved in a war between the Russian Army and the Ukrainian Army, so the whole place had become unreachable during the following years. It still was nowadays, unfortunately... From time to time, new battles had taken place in that territory, and no one from abroad could visit the village where that resort had once been located. Provided the resort even still existed.

Whatever the reason for her present conditions, Marisa had suffered deeply because of what she had undergone. Every time the fission happened, she had to move away, change her town and her country, so she could live mostly unnoticed and remain unseen. However, it was never easy to stay safe, eking out a living in the modern world without a good job, or enough resources to keep her comfortable, in the end. The woman had always been on the move, or better, on the run, for years, and she had never found a way to simply move back home. And no matter how hard she tried, of course she couldn't imagine ever being able to live in her hometown again, one day...

So, having no chance to visit his home, as she was afraid that her small town was under surveillance and she might be taken if spotted nearby, she just kept living alone, moving from one country to another. There was only one place, or better many places, where the woman could go whenever she wanted, as she was sure that no one would ever be close enough to see her features: the sites of her four graves, because no one would have thought of looking for her there. So she hoped, anyway...

Regretfully, she always found wise not to publicly display the fact that she had been there, so she wasn't able to leave some flowers on the ground near the small statue, or where this tomb of hers was situated, because she didn't want to leave any traces behind. After all, if such things were discovered at the feet of one of her many graves, someone might notice them and decide to put those gravesites under surveillance as well.

What Marisa wanted was for her tombs, at least, to remain safe. She liked the fact that she could go there, whenever she liked, to pay a visit to her dead remains. Well, the remains of her previous bodies...

So, it was during those brief moments that she could stay in silence, and be alone just with herself. Actually, the herself that she was now, and the corpse of herself that still lay underground, in that grave. Certainly she would like to be, in a way, with all the other copies of herself that lay in different tombs, and in different towns. But she was the only one living copy of herself, while her remains were many...four so far.

And, if things kept going that way, she thought with a fearful expression of how many dead copies of herself might be buried underground one day, as the fission seemed to happened every three years, and had no indication of stopping.

One day there might be too many dead copies of herself for Marisa to visit them all over the course of a single year...

These sad thoughts filled the woman's mind as she finally decided to move away from the tomb where she had stood before for a while.

"Did you come here to pay a visit to some parents?" The old voice seemed to come out of nothing, and almost scared the woman.

"No" the dejected Marisa replied, in a wary look. Who could be sure that it wasn't somebody watching over her movements even here? *You can be sure about no one, ever,* she told herself. Though, from the appearance she saw, that one just seemed to be a sweeper "I just had to see again the tomb of someone I knew." Certainly, the man couldn't say that it was her previous herself the one who lay below the ground in that grave of course.

"So, my deep condolences..." the other said, and kept cleaning the floor.

"Thanks for your words, man." Marisa said, as her steps were taking her elsewhere. To a place where she could really be alone and think on her unbelievable conditions.

If her studies were correct, and they had proved right four times so far, tomorrow would be another day for the oncoming, unwanted fission. And there was nothing she could do about it...

As it had previously happened, after tomorrow another dead copy of hers would drop to the ground somewhere. She would do her best to provide her next dead remains with a good funeral, as always. And she never forgot any of her copies that had passed away, as they were all well engraved in her memory.

After tomorrow, she would have just another grave to take care of, and to visit, from time to time... So Marisa reminded herself of those words from the famous writer named Isaac Asimov: "Life is pleasant. Death is peaceful. It's the transition that's troublesome."

How much truth was in those sentences! And the next transition was all that Marisa could think about as she left the cemetery behind her on her way out.

In fact, that old Sebastyne's quote about death did not apply to her. "You'll live for as long as you live, and once you stop living, you won't need to worry about staying alive any longer because you'll be dead."

Sebastyne could not have been more wrong, the woman uttered in a low tone. *Well, maybe not for all the others.* But that saying was wrong about her, for sure...

THE END

Dance Ballerina Dance
by Timothy Wilkie

Pretend you are dead and you will see who
really loves you.
                        African proverb.....

Some of the demons have left me now. Some are just sleeping when the Willow Cat perches on the fire escape and he makes his moaning sound the bad feelings return. Once a proud beat drifted down these city streets.

What if I get shot?

What if I don't?

I watch as a strange little bugs crawls up my arms. I think it is not the creatures in the bush it is the demons within us. The light of beauty lives in the words of freedom. My heart lies buried in the pavement of these lonely side streets. I stalk the sidewalks of my ancestors.

As I wait on the fire escape the sun rises and rushes down the streets and lingers in the sacred spaces. The train rushes by visible for an instant before it disappears underground. I see a time when my children will look down on planes as they fly by. There are no woodland shade or chilly summer nights. Death without tears lingers around every corner and a desperate kind of passion waits on the rooftops.

City trees I watch you stand against the noise and I've watched you when the wind has come and the snow has fallen and I know the sound of your despair. In a soiled sweat shirt I sit on this greasy old fire escape and await the dawn.

Through blinds partly closed I watch you dance The Nut Cracker as you whirl around and bound into the air. I know you from the name on your mailbox Dorthy Sanders, but you don't know me. Yet every morning I wake up before dawn to watch you dance. Dance ballerina dance.

My Mother sat in her chair for years after her stroke right in front of this window. I wonder if she watched you dance? The show was over for her one day while I was at work and I came home to find her slumped over in her seat.

She performed for over fifty years as a single parent. Every night she did her dance through the city with her rag-mop in hand and dumped trash cans and emptied ashtrays, until her curtain call, so I could go to school and learn to paint. She would smile at me when she said. "You have the gift." And I most certainly do, I have the gift of chaos.

Sometimes I wonder how she would paint her life? Deep strokes and sweeping realities or light and airy in watercolor? Dusty pastels or sharp pencil lines what would it all mean? An artist's rendition of the painted word "REGRET."

The sounds of the city mounts as the day grows brighter soon a thousand bodies will collide on the city sidewalks and I will be among them unnoticed they will not care for me like my Mother once did. Still the ballerina dances in silence and I watch unnoticed because she chooses not to see me. I speak to her in a thousand voices in my head but she replies with none.

It is the season of the bitch I tell myself and she mocks me with her silence as my rage simmers on a low fire. Unheard is the beggar's howl. "Did you not hear one tender moan in all your music?" I say, "for that was me. Your spirit must be taught to fear." I scream.

Across the rooftops thick probing fingers and chimney stacks my voice rings out. Looking down at the people on the sidewalks below I see too many ruins. Steadily they move along while their pointless lives reek of desperation like mine. Alone in their misery. It is sad to watch a species die on the holidays.

Dance my little ballerina dance, but all except a few have diseases like men and will die and never rise again. There is another way for I am Raven and I avoid the direct light of day. The Devil waits on Eighth and Broadway once the sun has gone away.

A sad old drunk dances across the street moving against the light and for a moment he smiles just before the truck driver checking his phone sends him directly to hell. The screams and the cries of passer by just motivate the dancer to dizzying heights. Dance ballerina dance you pirouette like an angel in flight.

She dances that fine line between want and desire and she is strong but I am not.

Darkness, darkness as my memory circles around me like a bloated insect and I count the children on the stoop. There are five just like every other day. They will wait there like a flock of birds until the time come s to take flight and then they will scatter to the four winds into the night.

In this jungle that I live there are no snakes yet the venom burns. There are no lions or tigers yet predators abound and death lay in wait for us all. The poison glitters, glistens, and shimmers as the hours unfold. Her hello would be the ending I was seeking as lizard cars their radiators grinning fill the streets to the brim. Cat-black tongues run up the alleyways with yellow teeth and mouths shut.

Dance ballerina dance for you are the lights and the delights and everything else that makes the holidays right. A rumor of war goes unheeded as the world all around me smells of automobile exhaust and the clouds slowly conceal the sunlight as the day drifts to shades of gray.

I see the shadows where others see only light. A quart can't hold a gallon if it hold a quart it's doing the best it can. Pity that the cats can't teach caution to the rats. Where once a spring flowed now sewage goes.

The bump and grind forever feeds my blood and warms my heart. The strident trains that speed the masses. I am lost! A lonely heart will take to the sea but I have lost myself in eternity. Dance ballerina dance take me apart to see how I work then maybe you'll understand my pain. For tonight I go to the tombs and steal another child from your womb and ride the subway trains.

Yule Only Live Twice
by A.R. Carpenter

Evil Doctor Scrooge had to be stopped before he ruined Christmas. Louisa Orange, agent of F.I.G., knew this as she crouched behind the tank of jet fuel, but as she took a sneaky look out at the propeller driven aircraft getting ready to take off from Scroogle's secret cave lair, she was having difficulty planting the bomb in the cargo hold. Namely because of the large number of guards in the way.

If the aircraft took off, there would be thousands of plastic explosive containing crackers winging their way to British shops. That just would not be very jolly. Especially when it came to the product recalls.

"You know, I can distract them", came a suave voice behind her.

She turned around and were it not for her training in remaining calm amid the unexpected, she would have dropped her pistol. She was facing a tuxedo wearing man with short black hair, a roguish smile and a raw physicality that would attract most humans of whatever sexual persuasion.

"Sorry, who are you?" she whispered in shock.

"The name's Fox. David Fox. Now if I go around to the back, they'll all be distracted. You can then run across and put the time bomb in the hold."

"Where do you come from?"

"I'll tell you later. At the Sandoval Bar. Now, darling, let me get on with this."

"Darling? What year is this? 1958?"

Fox wasn't responding. In fact, he'd disappeared... then she heard a couple of shouts from the guards. Followed by the sound of them opening fire at something.

She then saw David Fox casually walking towards the aircraft, vast swathes of ammunition heading in his direction, but everything was missing him. Surely, he couldn't avoid being shot?

Never mind. Time to go.

With the guards thoroughly distracted, she quickly cleared the distance to the aircraft. The door to the cargo bay was opened. She pulled out the explosive bauble from her bag, turned the timer to 10 minutes, pulled out the safety pin.

Then she tossed it among the crates of deadly crackers and started to run back. A quick glance at David. He was not only still standing; he was standing still and casually lighting a cigarette.

Louisa had no time to get to him. He would have to make his own way out.

* * * *

She got out of the cave just as the bomb detonated and the chain reaction ripped its way through Scrooge's Humbug Lair. A huge fireball blew its way out of the entrance, but she leapt clear and once the cacophony of the explosion had stopped reverberating, she got back to her feet.

"So, his goose is cooked," she said to the open air. Then there was a cackle behind her.

"Not so fast, Orange!"

She turned to see Doctor Scrooge standing behind her, holding a candy cane machine gun. One shot with that and she'd be missing her giblets every Christmas from now one.

"It's over, Scrooge," she said, watching his big red nose and wishing that she could just punch it. Unfortunately, she was too far away from that... and her pistol had fallen just out of her reach.

"You may have stopped my plan, but now I will stop you!"

At that point, she saw Fox coming behind Scrooge. Still looking completely unflappable.

How had he gotten out?

"Scrooge, Christmas Past is behind you!" Fox said.

Scrooge swung around, fired his weapon. Thick dust flew up everywhere. In the confusion,

Louisa moved to her side, grabbed her pistol and fired it squarely into his back. Scrooge slumped to the ground.

"And a partridge in a pear tree!" she yelled, then realised that she could have done a much better one-liner.

The dust cleared, but Fox was nowhere to be seen.

* * * *

Two days later, Louisa completed her report to her boss, the head of F.I.G.

"David Fox?" Sir Nick asked, "You must be completely insane. David Fox died in 1968. Heart attack after turkey with extra trimmings. Always ate, drank and smoked too much. Then there were all the girls..."

"Right... what's the Sandoval Bar?" Louisa asked.

"Old F.I.G. terminology for dying. The Sandoval Bar was destroyed in an air raid in 1941. Haven't used that for years though..."

"Sir. Request permission for a long vacation. I think I've seen a ghost."

The Gifts of the Season
by P. McCarthy

Twilight was falling and it was Isaac's favorite time of day. Two warm brown eyes quietly watched from the stoop of an empty storefront as Isaac fished something out from the depths of a city trashcan. Emblazoned on the front of the green barrel, 'Philadelphia – City of Brotherly Love.' In Isaac's opinion, this city was anything but full of love; lots of discord and crime, but love for him was hard to come by these days. In an instant, the warm brown eyes that watched him were at his side, a stray like himself that no one wanted. Bleak and frigid that day, the skies bulged swollen and gray and it looked like snow coming. Isaac noticed the unkempt dog by his side, feeling sorry for it, and shivered from the cold winds whistling through the buildings. His gnarled hand swiped across his purple lips. The sad state of the dog was getting to him. He pulled his threadbare coat tighter, as he walked away down the cobblestoned avenue doing his best to ignore the poor animal. The stray followed, his droopy eyes seemingly pleading in hopes that Isaac would share a bite of whatever he fished out of the city's trashcan or drop a few crumbs for him to lap up. Isaac's stomach grumbled loudly inspecting the jackpot he'd found. It was almost a full hotdog with all the fix in's on the menu with only a small bite taken out. The meat and bun were rock-solid frozen, but hunger doesn't need heated up to satiate an appetite. It puzzled the old man how people are so cavalier about throwing stuff away. Even still, he felt gratitude that they lack appreciation for the small things because it helps him survive, especially this time of year when folks are outside less because of the intolerable cold.

On that unusually bitter day in early November when Isaac snagged his sustenance out of the trash, the stray followed closely, his droopy eyes still eyeing the frozen delight as he trailed a few feet behind, hoping for an errant crumb. Isaac's joy over his lunch collapsed into sadness and compassion. How could he refuse that wretched face trailing alongside him; he knew what extreme hunger looked like and this old boy looked close to starving, his skeleton protruding underneath loose skin, which added to the poor dog's depressed look. He ended up feeding most of the hotdog to the poor thing, who dragged long ears and stubby legs along the trash-freckled cement and who, as hungry as he was, gingerly licked at the hotdog at first, not sure whether it was his to enjoy; at least that's what Isaac thought of the dog's behavior. As Isaac encouraged him to eat, knowing an empty stomach hurts when food is introduced, he patiently held the food for the dog as he nibbled, and once the old dog got a taste for eating again, he woofed the rest down. He lifted his wrinkly face to the old man, droopy eyes glistening, a whimper escaping his throat as his tongue licked the vestiges of flavor off his muzzle. Although hungry himself, Isaac was smitten; and for the old mutt, it was love at first bite, and they've been inseparable ever since. "I think ya look like a Barney. Is this what I should call ya, ol' boy? Barney? Ya like it?" His crinkled brown hand scratched behind Barney's droopy matted ears.

Barney's stubby tail helicoptered behind him, his back end bouncing over the frigid pavement as much as a starving dog can bounce and Isaac felt he made a good choice since the old boy seemed to respond to his new name.

Now, they scavenge together hoping to find something to eat at least once a day, twice if they're really lucky and the weather holds out. When the skies deepen to golden pinks and fuchsia purples and the sun dips behind the hi-rises, they trudge back with frozen, leaden legs to the hovel that Isaac built what seems forever ago now, hidden in a deep alley along with thirty other stray humans that no one wants.

He considered himself blessed one day soon after he found himself homeless, lost and alone amid the many nameless hordes walking the city's streets digging through trashcans, an unfortunate side effect of losing both his wife to a battle with cancer and his position at the candy factory in the same month. A position he held his entire lifetime, but the new corporation wasn't interested in his tenure, he was only an old number and they didn't take kindly to the many weeks of his absence. He tried to force himself to attend day after day, but the loss of his wife of fifty-two years was too much to bear, and found comfort in the depths of a strong malt whiskey. It was the only way to assuage his pain. The long-standing factory on Germantown handed him his pink slip and denied him unemployment benefits claiming alcoholism as the source of letting him go. He tried to fight against the politics of the company and lost miserably, the little money he had dwindled away to a pauper's wallet. At his age, no one would hire him – no one wanted a man of seventy-two starting over. He floated on what he had left in the bank, which after paying his wife's medical bills wasn't much, and eventually he just couldn't keep up any longer. Social Security wasn't enough to maintain his monthly debt and the bank foreclosed on their menial row home; and one they'd lovingly built together over the long hardworking and wearying years of their lives together. He had no family left, a curse for living to seventy-two. He outlived everyone who ever meant something to him, including his lifelong friends. Misery seemed to be his armor and he bore it like a warrior with nary a complaint for his plight.

One day soon after misfortune turned her dour, heartless eyes on the poor soul, he aimlessly wandered through his old neighborhood reliving past memories of his lifetime that caused his yellowed eyes to tear, his heart aching. A bottle sunk low, hidden in a crinkly paper bag inside a pocket of the only winter apparel he possessed helped to ease memories flooding his mind. That day, he stumbled upon a jackpot and felt hope for the first time in weeks. Someone had discarded a huge refrigerator box on the curb. Isaac seized it quickly before someone else took it and with arthritic hands, slowly dragged the oversized box to the alley where he slept wrapped in newspaper every night to keep himself warm. It took him the entire day to get it from his old neighborhood through the dark and treacherous streets to his alley, but that first night with his new box, was the first night that late September just over a year ago that he had a real shelter as he slid between the folds of the box. It was like living in the Taj Mahal. The warmth was luxurious.

He told himself that the exercise was

good for him roaming about the city and its suburbs when the arthritis wasn't acting up, but the truth for him was, he was on quests for survival gear. Shortly after he found the box, he snagged wads of painters' drop cloths from someone's trash bin, and another excursion, he found rolls of discarded plastic sheets, *and* he found another refrigerator box. He hurried back to his box-home and came up with a plan to construct an actual shelter for himself instead of laying between the folds of the thick cardboard. On his journeys, he kept a close eye on the cement and tar of the streets looking for chewed gum and scooped wads of disgusting goo out of trashcans. It became his poor man's plaster to paste and stick his boxes, cloths and plastic together to create a warmish and mostly waterproof domicile of sorts. Night after frigid night, his poor man's shelter became more comfortable, warmer and a lucky find of an old oil lantern gave him light to read discarded magazines and newspapers by. After finishing them, he repurposed them to line the inside of his box for an added layer of warmth. By the time Barney found this sensitive soul, Isaac had the shelter finished, which was big enough for the two of them and Isaac was happy for the old boy's company. Barney gave him a purpose and he reveled in taking care of him.

Most days, the two set off to their favorite park; and Isaac always carried the large, black umbrella he fished out of someone's garbage for a couple of reasons. Even though the umbrella was tattered and mostly useless in defense against the rain, it was more a walking stick for the old man and a weapon for his and Barney's protection; the metal spike at the tip came to a perfect point, if not a little rusty.

Just off the Boulevard, the park was a good-sized patch, not too big, nor too small and had comfortable benches and many pine trees lining the perimeter and all throughout to protect them from the elements. Edging the park was a homey tree-lined U-shaped street the park sat between where warm-looking and inviting two-story brick homes gave the green pasture where they sat all day, a cul-de-sac feel and Isaac felt secure resting there. No one ever seemed to mind that he and Barney sat in the park all day, and if they did, no one ever said anything to them. The first visit by the police officers driving by almost caused Isaac's heart to stop; he had no proper leash for Barney, only a short rope for a lead; not that he ever used it, and more important, he had no license for his companion. They asked about his reason for being there, stating there was a 'no loitering' policy throughout the city, which scared Isaac, as he wiped his hand across his wrinkled lips. He thought he was going to lose Barney and that he'd have no place to go during the day, so he shared his story of what happened to him and how he came to find himself homeless. Max and Nicky, as the policemen became known, at first seemed to think his story was malarkey, just another bum living on the streets, until their next visit a few days' later. Maybe they'd verified the circumstances of his story and decided a harmless old man with a dog sitting in the park wasn't such a terrible thing since they didn't cause any trouble and no one's reported them, and maybe they took pity on the unfortunate soul and his companion. Whatever the case, it took only a few weeks before Isaac, Barney and the Police Officers were on a first name basis, the cops' even bringing hot coffee for Isaac, sometimes a hot meal, and dog biscuits for old Barney. For the first time in a long while, Isaac made new friends and didn't feel quite so alone and in need of human conversation, even though he'd had many one-sided conversations with his furry companion. Barney finally knew what it was like to live a somewhat normal life, and grew used to getting a daily biscuit from his police friends, his tail a propeller whenever he spied Max and Nicky pulling up to the curb.

In the late spring, summer and most of

autumn, life wasn't too tough for them since there weren't many challenges dealing with the outside elements other than rain, but that feels good more often than not. Isaac looks at it as a free shower. His mantras over the many years *learn to dance in the rain* keeps his outlook towards his circumstances positive and bearable, still not complaining. Sometimes, apart from missing the creature comforts of having a house, it almost feels like a blessing being outdoors enjoying the gifts that God gives to him. During the nicer months weather-wise, the park and ballfield are in full swing; always children and sometimes adults swinging away, batting their baseballs, softballs, or throwing Frisbees and old Barney even pitches in to help when a stray comes flying over the fence, his stubby little legs running to fetch it and deliver it back to their owners. He seems to enjoy retrieving the balls and doesn't mind the occasional run. The players have taken to *expecting* him to help and have begun carrying treats to reward him for his effort, which makes Barney even more agreeable to pitch in! Isaac enjoys these moments, watching life go on around him, almost as if he's watching a movie, and seeing his old companion acting like a puppy again, he smiles as he enjoys the warmth of the sun and gentle breezes that cool his skin. When the sun begins to wane, he and

Barney head back to their shelter in the alley, umbrella for protection tightened in his gnarled grip, wanting to keep them safe, knowing it was a good day forgetting their circumstances if only for a while.

The cold weather poses more challenges to them, as their arthritic bones and creaking joints find it harder to tolerate the chilly air, but it's also Isaac's favorite time of year. This November is unusually cold and frosty and whether it's Isaac's body that is growing more intolerable of the cold, or the fact that he's getting too old to be homeless is anyone's guess, but his thoughts have begun to think of ways to find a home for both himself and his beloved pet. Knowing you want to have a home, and being able to secure one are far different things, and Isaac knows it's a pipe dream and that he's probably going to die on the streets. His only hope is that Barney will survive without him. The thought of Barney having to struggle through this life without Isaac to take care of him makes him cry. He thinks *what a pathetic picture I must be, an old man sitting in public, crying,* but he knows Barney probably won't make it out here on his own and it breaks his heart.

Even with the days growing shorter, and the nights much colder he feels no hurry to get back to their shelter. He enjoys staying on his park bench with the old boy snuggled next to him on a blanket they scrounged from a trash bin along the way. He watches with yellowed watery eyes, old age slowing his blinking, a small smile on his purpling lips as the sun wanes in the sky and the lamplights begin glowing from behind every window shade in the houses around the circle. Every day is the same for them, though getting back to the alley they call, 'home' becomes more treacherous as the nights grow darker earlier.

~

Another Thanksgiving is upon Isaac and Barney, and they still occupy the old wood planks. Cold as they may be, the thought of spending the entire night in their box is unappealing. Their stomach's bloated, they had a delicious hot meal and even dessert this Thanksgiving thanks to a great many of the neighborhood's people who've come to know them through the warmer months and brought them food. So many generous souls gave them food that day that they had a few bags to take home that night. There was enough to share with his mates in the alley and still more, which lasted quite a few days, and he and Barney were so grateful for everyone's kindness. Smiles were aplenty this Thanksgiving thanks to the kind folks' generosity in the neighborhood.

The next evening, still full from all the food given them, Isaac and Barney sat quietly on their favorite park bench bundled in blankets, and as the sun lowered and lights came on behind darkened windows, Isaac watched shadow puppets of everyone behind their drawn shades as they returned home from Black Friday shopping. He imagined what their lives might look like on the other side of those windows, and felt melancholy for his own life behind his own shades that seems a lifetime ago.

He envisioned some would be sitting down to a hot supper with their family, (perhaps turkey leftovers,) and others watching the television. Some may be sitting quietly reading a book, or listening to music and enjoying a glass of wine, or maybe even putting up their Christmas trees. Were some having an argument or playing board games with their children? Were they making vacation plans for the summer, excitedly making holiday plans for Christmas, or helping with homework? Was there an elderly person like himself sitting alone and silently wishing for another soul to spend time with them? He thought back to once upon a time, not so long ago, when he had his beautiful wife, Mary to enjoy a meal with, or laugh at some crazy TV show they'd watched together. He remembered them looking forward to Halloween every year, handing out candy to all the neighborhood kiddies, remarking how wonderful a costume they wore, knowing it was the start of the holiday season. Every year, after Trick-or-Treat ended, they'd bundle up and go for a walk through their neighborhood to look at everyone's scary decorations, hand in hand as they slowly trod the city's streets to buy a caramel apple taffy, and hot cider. He never imagined one day he'd be left to walk those same streets alone in the not-too-distant-future, sad, scared, and unsure of what tomorrow will bring but he sensed Mary walked those streets with him still.

He recalled the banquets they had on their own Thanksgivings when friends and their small family came to gather for the harvest. They shared the day together watching football while the women prepared the feast, the fragrance of turkey, filling, greens with pork, baked rolls, and sweet potato pies tantalized their senses until the magic moment when they all sat to hold hands in prayer. Such lovely memories, but Isaac can't make complaint even though he finds himself alone because at least he had it for a time. Some will never know those joys and his heart is sad for them. The fragrance of wood burning somewhere near him pulls him from his memories. Looking across at the circle of houses, he sees smoke billowing from several chimneys, and then realizes he isn't alone, he has Barney by his side now, but he can't stop the sadness that breaks his heart knowing one day Barney may be gone too, and he'll be all alone again, the pain too great to hold his tears back.

Barney became alarmed when Isaac cried and snuggled closer to his human's side, and Isaac cried harder still, the foresight of pain to come too great to squelch. His heart ached for his beloved dog already, even though he remained faithfully by his side. Drooping brown eyes full of love and a sadness of their own tipped backwards to gaze at his human, love and concern on his sweet wrinkly face. Isaac smiled through his teardrops and reached an arthritic hand to the side of Barney's face rubbing his flabby jowls, cooing to him. "I'm alright sweet boy. Your ol' pap is jus' fine, jus' sad is all. Don't you worry ol' boy, papa's alright, and we gonna be okay – together." Barney slowly gave Isaac's hand one loving lick and went back under the blanket, falling asleep again.

~

Everyone's attention was turning to the Christmas season, and this was truly Isaac's very favorite time of year. True, he was so much colder, but he couldn't help but walk through the city to view the lights just as he and his lovely wife used to do every Christmas season. They'd walk, oohing, and aahing over everyone's decorations, and stop for hot chocolate and roasted chestnuts on the avenue as they took in the season so alive with love, lights, and music and he couldn't help but want to be a part of it still. It's an homage to his Mary. Poor Barney trudged dutifully along, happy to oblige his human, even though Isaac could see he was wearing down. His stubby little legs struggled to keep up, a stumble or two and a near fall when he couldn't muster a curb caused Isaac great distress and concern.

It's been almost a week since Thanksgiving and misfortune once again turned her compassionless eyes on Isaac. He and Barney were making their way to the park on an extremely cold and blustery day. Frosty mist that was not quite snow created quite the snarls in traffic all around the city, as streets would wet and then turn slick with iciness. Sirens were rampant this day as one vehicle after the other slid into another, most traveling too quickly on the already slick cobblestones.

At a crosswalk, Isaac pushed the stoplight's button to give him the right-of-way so he and Barney could safely cross the avenue.

Either the light malfunctioned, or he misread the traffic light as he stepped off the curb onto the slick avenue and nearly lost his footing, but he managed not to fall. Barney walked alongside him on the side of oncoming traffic. A car veered off the center of its lane and headed straight for Barney. Isaac tried to pull Barney out of the path of the runaway car hydroplaning over the iced surface but it all happened so quickly. The eyes of the driver locked with Isaac's eyes, both screaming in horror as his beloved Barney shrieked in pain when the car rolled over him. The old man collapsed next to his beautiful boy when the car continued up and over the curb and rammed into the traffic light.

The driver flew out of his car, tears streaming down his face and on shaky legs, his body trembling, ran to their sides. He checked Isaac first who was moaning and cooing to Barney who laid whimpering and breathing shallow. Blood flowed from open wounds on his back end, his hind legs slightly twisted, as he lay still. Isaac knew this was it; today he'd loose his beloved companion.

Sirens screeched as police and medics swarmed the scene. The driver of the car was talking with the police when Max and Nicky pulled up to the scene. Isaac still lay on the wet road next to Barney, saying his farewells to his precious boy. Max and Nicky spoke briefly to the driver, came to Isaac and his companion, and checked Barney's injuries. Seeing the pain the old boy was in, both Officers cried, offering comfort to Isaac.

Isaac was surprised when Paramedics wheeled a gurney towards them and carefully lifted Barney on the stretcher. He began to protest, when they explained, as they looked Barney over, that his injuries might be survivable and that the driver offered to pay all the expenses. They told him they were taking him to the animal hospital and offered for Isaac to ride with them so he could be with his dog. He climbed in the back of the ambulance to comfort his ol' boy. Tears of worry and gratitude flowed freely . . .

~

Isaac loved sitting in his favorite park, on his favorite bench with his beloved Barney snuggled under the two blankets he carted along, one to sit on and one to cover. He felt so blessed to have two now. He saw it as God's Christmas gift to them, even if he found it in someone's trashcan on the way to the park one fortunate day. One man's trash, another's treasure is what his momma always said of trash-picking treasures when he was little, as she set out a 'new-to-them' piece of china for their holiday meal.

The Church down at the opposite corner of the park was having a musical chorus this Christmas Eve, and as he and Barney snuggled under their blanket, a canopy of glittering stars brightly lit the indigo sky overhead. The air was icy and sweet smelling, and the scent of chestnuts roasting hung in the crisp air and Isaac felt completely at peace as the voices of angels began rolling across the park in echoing waves reaching his ears, sacred Christmas carols sung in the sweetest tones. Barney howled gently as the melodies washed over them and Isaac cried, scratching the old boy behind his ears, watching his beloved companion bring honor and glory to the blessed baby. He hummed along himself, his old voice scratchy and worn as tears frosted on his weathered cheekbones. "Sing to the ba-bee, old boy. Go on an' feel the joy!"

He thought about that week just after Thanksgiving when he was certain he'd lost his precious boy. The memory was hazy where the actual accident was concerned but the aftermath was something he'd never forget. He leaned his head back, his hand swiping across his chapped lips, the music filling his ears, and all that Barney went through filled his thoughts. He felt nothing but gratitude for the driver of the car, Timothy, who's become a good friend to them, and all that Max and Nicky did for them too. Timothy feeling terrible over the accident, visited Barney and Isaac every day in the Animal Hospital while Barney was recovering to make sure they had everything they needed, and even rented a motel room near the hospital for Isaac so he could be near his companion as long as it took Barney to heal. Isaac's heart swelled with gratitude for Timothy.

Barney had suffered two broken hind legs, and his hips and pelvis were broken too from the impact. The open wounds were severely infected and needed abraded twice daily to heal the infections, along with multiple courses of antibiotics. It was an arduous, painful recovery for the ol' boy and Isaac had no clue how he was going to care for Barney after his release. Worry consumed his mind.

The Doctors were ready to release Barney from the hospital after being there for two and a half weeks, even though Barney's hind legs were still in casts. He still struggled with walking and it was obvious the poor little guy was still in a great deal of pain. Max and Nicky visited as often as they could since the accident happened, and brought donations of food, toiletries, clothes, and money for Isaac's comfort and support. The day before Barney was set to go home, which for him was back to the streets, Max and Nicky came to visit and they had a surprise for the two homeless castoffs.

Max popped his head in the doorway first.

"Hey you two, how's it going today, how's the little patient?" His demeanor was unusually cheerful; a twinkle glimmered in his eyes as he approached to give Barney a good petting, and shook the old man's hand. The dog's tail turned into a gently spinning propeller.

"Max! It's so good ta see ya. Our patient's getting along fine, but the doc's ready to send 'im home tomorrow, and I don't mind sayin', I'm worried how I'm gonna take care of 'im on the streets, although, the good Man upstairs has taken care of us this long, I s'pose he's got us covered once they let Barney go home.

"Ah, well my friend, Nicky and I got some news on that front!"

As soon as Max said that, Nicky popped through the doorway. Behind him, he pulled a red Radio Flyer wagon with wooden sides and a tailgate that drops down for loading. "Hey everyone, Santa's come early for you two!"

Isaac's jaw dropped down, his eyes welled with tears. His gnarled hand rubbed across his purpling lips, just as he always does when he tries to hide his emotions, or feels stress. Tears wove through the lines of his aged face. Overcome, he barely managed to squeak out, "Ya'll boys are such a blessin' ta us, and I don't know how ta thank ya."

"No need my friend," Max said softly, his own eyes welling with liquid, "Nicky and me," he nodded, smiling in Nicky's direction, "we've been out collecting donations for you guys from all the neighborhoods we troll. Funny thing is, as we were asking for donations for you two, even neighborhoods across the city have heard of you both. It's amazing how many people know about yous guys. Nearly everyone we talked to were more than willing to donate something to help you two. I ain't never seen anything like it before! Huh, Nicky?"

"I never seen a reaction like that either," Nicky proffered. "People's kindness and generosity just blew us away, and here you have a part of what the donations have purchased," he nodded towards the wagon.

Isaac's head reeled back. "A part of the donations? Dis is more than enough for Barney and me ta get along out there; what more could we need? We're so grateful ta everyone and ta ya both for doin' this for us. How can we ever repay ya's?" He hung his head and bawled openly for a few minutes, overwhelmed with emotions.

Max piped up, "Well Isaac, we have to

tell you," he was out of breath from his excitement, "there's more, but we're not gonna tell you about it til Barney here is released. What time is the doc letting him go, do you know?"

Isaac wiped his eyes with the sleeve of his 'new-to-him' thermal shirt that Timothy bought for him. "I believe he said we'd be outta here 'round eleven tomorrow morn."

"Then we'll be here to pick yous up," they both said in unison, excitement dancing in their eyes. They said their 'goodbyes' and went off to work their shift.

Isaac sat stroking Barney, stunned into silence and deep thought trying to figure out what was going on. Barney lay licking his hand, his tail gently wagging.

"Looks like we get ta go home tomorrow, boy, ya ready to go home?"

The dog's tail thumped the padded table where he lay . . .

~

Nicky and Max arrived right at eleven the next day and helped Isaac get Barney ready to head back to the streets. They struggled to get him aboard the wagon, and though he was scared, once they tucked him in with his blankie, he settled and seemed to enjoy the ride out of the hospital. Isaac felt relief that Barney didn't have to try to walk the distance yet.

From the back seat, Isaac spoke up. "I ain't been in the back of a police cruiser since I was a kid, and it sho feels weird to be back here."

"What were you in a police cruiser for?" Max asked with laughter in his voice. "You seem like a stand-up guy."

"Momma was teaching me a lesson after I stole Bazooka Joe from the Five & Dime on the corner of Germantown and Seymour. She called the po-lice on me and got me arrested for stealing the penny candy. I was never so scairt in my life, I can tell ya, but it taught me a good lesson and I ain't never took nuthin' since that didn't belong ta me! She was a smart lady, my momma. That was a good lesson she taught this ol' man!"

Isaac noticed as they twisted and turned through street after street that they weren't heading in the right direction back to the alley he and Barney call, 'home'.

"Guys, mind if I ask ya's where we're headin'? This ain't the way ta my alley."

"Sit tight, my friend," Nicky chimed, turning around to smile brightly at Isaac, "it's a part of the surprise we have for you both!"

He settled his head against the back of the

seat and closed his eyes for a few minutes, already tired from the excitement of the day, but knew these guys were good men and wouldn't do him harm. It'd been a long time since he trusted anybody, but in his heart, and after everything they've done for them, he knew he could trust his new friends. The car gently rocked him into a twilight sleep as he thought they probably found a shelter where they could stay while his little companion finished healing. His gnarled hand gently stroked a sleeping and contented Barney as he drifted off to sleep, the voices of his friends chatting in the front seat fading.

It started to sleet when the car finally came to a stop, waking both Isaac and Barney, who sleepily lifted his wrinkled face and stretched his furry neck, looking out the side window.

The street was familiar to Isaac but his brain was still foggy and not being fully awake, he wasn't able to process where he was. Max and Nicky exited the cruiser and opened the back door for Isaac who slowly climbed out of the car. He stood and stretched his muscles, trying to get his brain to work, while Nicky got the wagon out of the trunk for Barney.

Awareness dawned on Isaac. "Guys! This is my ol' street where I lived with my Mary! That right there," he pointed to a red faux brick-sided house in the middle of the block, "was my home! What in heaven's name we doin' here?"

Max was the first to answer. "Remember we said people all over the city have heard and know of the two of you, and that the wagon for Barney was only *part* of the donations we'd collected?"

"Yeah, I remember ya sayin' that, but what's that got ta do with bein' here?"

"Well," Nicky continued where Max left off, "this is the other part of all the donations we'd collected, and there's even more to tell you! First, there was enough to put a down payment on this house for you. Unfortunately it's not the one you used to live in, but that one there," he pointed at the end of the street, "that one there now belongs to you and Barney!"

"What in the good Lord's name? Is this fer real ya guys? I can't believe what ya's are sayin'! Am I hearin' ya right?"

They wheeled Barney through the front door, and set him carefully on the carpet. He stump-ran to a dog bed in the center of the front room and flopped down on it, and began to enjoy a bone laid along the edge, his tail flapping as he chewed. Isaac's hand repeatedly swiped across his lips as he slowly spun around taking in his new home, joy flowing through every part of him, still not believing this place belongs to him, and feeling so grateful to have a place to call home. In boxes sitting around the sparsely furnished room, sat his few belongings that he'd collected over his time on the streets. Tears streamed through the lines on his face as he stood and bawled; his gratitude too great to hold inside any longer. "Gentlemen," he said softly with a cracked, strained voice, "I don't know how ta ever say, thank ya enough for all the kindness the two of ya have shown ta me and my boy. You made a very ol' man so very happy, and I'm forever in your debt."

After taking a tour of his new home, the three of them sat at the turquoise Formica table in the small kitchen. His friends shared with him all that's happened while he and Barney spent their days in the animal hospital. They told him that an investigation was performed on the traffic light that Isaac thought he switched on the day of the accident, and that Investigator's from the City determined the accident happened due to the fault of the light malfunctioning. In other words, Timothy never stopped his car because the light never changed for him *to* stop, and the accident wasn't his fault, or anybody's fault. The City has reimbursed Timothy for all his expenses and settled out of Court with Isaac for all damages, which included them purchasing this home and enough cash for him and Barney to live out the rest of their days in comfort. Max and Nicky stood in for Isaac as proxies and sued the City on his behalf.

Isaac was dumbfounded and now understood why Max and Nicky only came to visit the hospital occasionally. Apparently, they were busy working *and* attending court hearings. He knew without a doubt, that they were the best friends he'd ever had!

~

From one of the homes across the park in the cul-de-sac, a couple practically dragged a curly haired girl dressed in a red coat and white patent-leather shoes with lace socks by them, and then they spun in a circle. "Merry Christmas, Isaac and Barney; we almost didn't see you two under those blankets!"

The wife pulled something from around her back and leaned over to Isaac, handing it to him. "Merry Christmas, Isaac, this is for you and Barney. We hope you like it, and may it bless you both."

The large box wrapped in red and gold paper, had a gold ribbon circling the box and a huge red bow on the top. "Thank ya kindly folks, that's mighty generous of ya! Barney and me are blessed; ain't we boy?" Isaac spoke, his voice betraying his surprise, tears springing to his eyes once more. He scratched the top of Barney's head with one hand, and wiped his palm across his cold lips with the other. He didn't move to unwrap the package, gratitude and embarrassment flowing through him. The couple shook his weathered glove, wished them another Merry Christmas and grasping the young girls' hand, who hid behind her daddy, rushed off towards the church.

Isaac, although grateful as he watched the family quickly walk towards the church, was in no hurry to open their gift. He set it aside on the wooden slats next to him, leaned his head against the bench, closed his eyes while resuming scratching Barney's ears, and allowed the angels' voices to wash over him. The melodies swirled inside his eardrums, Barney's guttural vocal utterances enhancing the heavenly experience. Isaac stared into the heavens silently praying. Crystal snow gently began to cascade from the sky, and soon came heavier; trees and grass alike bearing ornaments of fluffy, wet powder. Everything looked as if it was decorated now. He still didn't want to leave and laid his head back once more closing his eyes as Barney burrowed under the blanket to warm himself. The sweet music lulled them both to sleep as the fluffy crystals piled around them, mostly submerging them under their new white blanket made of snow.

Snowflakes matted on his eyelashes drawing Isaac from his sleep, the music still sweetly echoing through the park. Movement in the darkness drew his liquid eyes to the horizon across the park. He watched a small, dark figure trudging through the few inches of freshly falling snow laying over the ground. The Christmas lights winking in and out as she passed through their glow. As the figure grew nearer, he recognized it was a woman, her breath coming out in frosty puffs. He's seen her many times over the past year but still didn't know her name. Her house sat directly opposite where he and Barney perched on the bench. She always skirted around them, and Isaac felt that maybe she didn't like homeless people hanging around her neighborhood, but now here she is making a beeline for them. He wondered if maybe she'd finally steeled her nerve to ask them to leave, or perhaps she assumed he's been watching her home for an attempted burglary; whatever the reason, he knew all he could do was wait for her to arrive to find out what she wanted.

He watched quietly as she continued moving closer to them, studying her. She was an older woman, though most likely younger than he was, and noticed she wore a mid-length skirt and ankle boots. A red scarf wrapped her neck and her stylish coat buttoned to her chin, and closer still, he saw she wore fitted brown leather gloves to match her booties. She definitely had style. She carried something in the palm of her hand. She kept a close watch on him as she neared, and when within speaking distance she walked more confidently holding her free hand out to Isaac, her green eyes locked on his honeyed orbs.

"Hi, I'm Evie," her voice was bright and cheery. "You must be *the* Isaac and Barney all our neighbors are talking about, am I right?"

"Yes ma'am, ya sure are. Pleased to make your acquaintance, ma'am. Would you care to share our bench?" Isaac blushed, realizing it's not *their* bench at all, just one they borrow and occupy on a daily basis.

"Thanks no, and you hush with all that ma'am business, and call me Evie, if you would please. Ma'am makes me feel so old and no woman wants to feel old, even if they are." She giggled at her own levity.

"Well, I'm pleased ta meet ya, Evie. What brings ya out on such a cold night if I can ask? Ya are headin' to church?" Just then, Barney pushed his nose out from under the blanket.

Evie jumped just a bit, surprised. She

must've forgot Barney was there. "My, my, now aren't you just the most precious boy! Just look at that sad face of yours." She bent to pet his head, which Barney was happy to extend his neck to receive. "Truth told I wanted to come over to meet the two of you, and to bring you some of my world famous pumpkin cake with homemade cream cheese frosting, unless you both had your fill of it?"

"Oh no ma'am, I mean, Evie, neither of us have had that yet and it sounds might-ee fine," he said with glee as his hands reached for the package. "World famous, ya say?" Looking up into her face, he giggled a bit, which came out sounding giddy. His face turned red.

"Well, world famous in my opinion and just about half of Philly. I sell these to all the bakeries for Thanksgiving and Christmas, and every year, I have more and more people clamoring for them, I can't keep up sometimes."

"Well, I'm sure it's gonna be delicious, thank ya. This is so very nice of ya."

"It's my pleasure, I hope you enjoy it." Without missing a beat, she added, "Now, what would you say about having lunch with me?"

Isaac was confused, and it showed on his face.

"Whoops, where is my head, let me try that again. I've wanted to come over and say, 'hello' for a while now, but I haven't found the courage until now to talk to you. You see, I've been rather a loner ever since I lost my William a few years ago and I thought maybe Christmas Eve would be a nice time to introduce myself, so here I am!"

"I'm sorry for your loss, Evie. It's nice of ya ta come over ta meet us. I've seen ya around but I worried that maybe ya didn't take ta us sitting here every day; some people mind that kinda thing and well . . .," His voice trailed off and he blushed realizing he might have offended her.

"Oh now I've gone and done it, I've embarrassed you. I'm sorry, Isaac, that wasn't my intention. So, I guess I'll leave you both to it, and bid you so long, for now."

As she turned to leave, Isaac found his voice, and spoke quickly, "It wasn't you!"

Evie turned back to him, smiling and curious.

"Excuse me? Wasn't me?"

"I mean, *you* didn't embarrass me, *I* embarrassed me because I assumed ya didn't like homeless guys and their dogs hanging around the neighborhood, and yes, I'd love to meet you for lunch sometime. For the record so ya don't get scared over what I jus' said, Barney and me have our own home now and there's something else, but I don't really know what it is I feel. I can't seem to find the words, let alone understand what it is, maybe gratitude. Ya might be an answer ta my prayers. I don't know. Whatever it is, the answer is, yes, I'd like ta meet ya for lunch if I didn't scare ya away."

Evie waved his words away, "Oh, you didn't scare me, or offend me. At *my* age, it takes a lot more than that to ward me off! I'm glad you two have found a place to call home, but I actually already knew it. The entire neighborhood is buzzing about the two of you. I wanted to see for myself what all the fuss is about and I could already tell you seem to be a very good man. World needs more of you in it! Barney's welcome to come too; we can find a place with curbside seating if you'd like even though it's likely to be freezing outside. Sound good?"

"Yes ma'am, I mean Evie. Thank ya and that's so kind but I think it might be too much for him still. He'll be fine for a little while on his own at home, as long as we're not gone too long."

"Well, I suppose I should let you two get on with enjoying your Christmas Eve and I'm turning into an ice cube, and besides, I do want to catch some of the service. I promised myself I'd force myself to go for my husband's sake this year. You see, he was the churchgoer and I thought I'd do this in his honor, so . . ." She trailed off.

"I think that's a beautiful gesture and a wonderful way ta honor his memory. Enjoy the service Evie and Merry Christmas ta ya!"

~ ~ ~

The church service ended and Isaac decided it was time to head home. Taking one last look into the snowy sky, and giving a prayer of thanks, he helped Barney into his wagon, tucking him in with blankets so he'd stay warm. He was a good sport sharing his wagon with their Christmas present and pumpkin cake. They slowly made their way home through the nearly deserted streets as snow quietly fell blanketing the city. It was indeed a silent night and one of the most beautiful walks ever, and having the love of Barney to share this Christmas made his heart swell.

Towing the wagon behind him, he came to his stoop in front of his undecorated home and there was a Christmas tree fully decorated. A large tag hanging from a bough read, Merry Christmas Isaac and Barney!

He knew it was from the best friends in the world and smiled.

~

The following Christmas Eve, Isaac gave his time and donations to everyone who had need, returning the kindness that was given to him the year before; kindness that saved his life and Barney's too. He spent time at Mary's gravesite, talking long into the day with her and attended his church, even singing in the choir, his voice rough but filled with love and gratitude to his Lord in heaven for all the gifts he bestowed upon him.

Christmas Day found Isaac's home filled with his friends, Max, Nicky, and Timothy along with their wives and children, as well as Evie who proudly stood near Isaac's side wearing a sparkling engagement ring glowing on her finger, but Evie's face and the happiness in her soul glowed even brighter. Isaac felt fulfilled and happier than he knew he had a right to be as he puttered in the kitchen preparing the Christmas feast for his new family. The air was fragrant with turkey, filling, greens, and Evie's homemade pumpkin cake with cream cheese frosting.

Under the Christmas tree stood a manger, it was the gift given to he and Barney the year before wrapped in red and gold paper by the young couple. In the manger, lay the blessed babee in a cradle and lying next to the manger was a healthy, happy, and much loved Barney. His chin resting on his paws, his warm brown droopy eyes full of adoration staring at the tiny infant cradled among the moss, loved and warmed by the humblest animals.

LOVE ON THE RUN
By
Ben Rose

Chapter One

I was working in the kitchen, preparing Cobb Salads for dinner, when Ma flung open the screen door, out of breath, her cheeks flushed, sweat dripping from her forehead in spite of the bandana she wore.

"Stephanie, Doc and Billy need to speak with us in the front office. Caroline is already heading that way."

My eyes widened. "Something wrong?"

"Not wrong exactly, but you'll want to be sitting when they tell you."

I washed my hands, dried them on my jeans, and turned lunch preparation over to Jeanie and Rae, an eighteen-year-old couple who lived in the main house.

Ma and I scurried toward the large brick building that faced the community gate. Doc and Billy built this community in upstate Washington as a place for the protection of runaways, throwaways, survivors of domestic violence, and other marginalized members of society. My sister Caroline and I fit in to that third category, as does Ma.

As we approached the front porch, my eyes caught Caroline's. She was seated on a porch swing, dressed in overalls, a grey t-shirt and black, crap-spattered, work boots. She'd been tending to the horses on the back forty. Across from her, sitting in rocking chairs, were two middle-aged men to whom we owed our lives. Doc, dressed in formal attire, and a chestnut colored homburg, was puffing on an expensive cigar as usual. Beside him, Billy was dressed in black from head to toe. He sported black ditty-bop shades, and a black bandana around his shoulder length salt and pepper hair.

Ma and I sat beside Caroline, and Doc broke the news. "There was a young man of twenty-one years age who arrived this afternoon. He's had some legal troubles. He's clearly had a rough go of things."

"That's great," I shrugged as Billy lit a cigar. "So what's the urgency? How does it involve us? Other than that he's going to be a new resident?"

"Kid," Billy rubbed his chin, "he asked for you by name. With the last name Baker." I gasped. We'd changed our last name nine years ago. "What's his name?"

Ma gripped my arm. Caroline's eyes widened. A single rivulet of sweat swept down my spine. Doc puffed his cigar. "Vincenzo Cassiel Michelangelo Il-Cazzo."

My head swam, and my heart palpitated. "Vinnie? He's here? But...how?"

"So you know him?" Billy blew a plume of smoke.

"We did. For a brief time." Ma held me as tears trickled down my cheeks. "His people are the ones who freed us in the first place. They took us to safety."

I stood and walked to the railing. The pond was full of people swimming and skinny dipping, sunbathers lay on towels in the grass doing the rotisserie thing, there were workers building another cabin, and my mind was reeling back to a time when I was twelve years old.

* * *

Everyone has to be born and grow up somewhere. Harvest Junction was that place for me. A speck on the map in northern New England, if one were to attempt finding the exact location it would take a while. It was a nice enough place aesthetically, and, if not for my pa, it would have been a fine place to live forever.

I grew up the hard way for twelve years in that town. There were plenty of other kids, but Caroline and I rarely played with them. Pa expected us to do yard chores, help Ma cook and clean, and keep to ourselves in public. If we strayed from this path, Pa had no problem slapping us, kicking our butts, or taking a strap to us.

I was mowing the yard one day, two months after turning twelve, when a moving truck pulled in five houses down the block. A man in a dark blue pinstripe suit, and a woman dressed in green slacks and a daisy yellow blouse followed behind in a minivan. With them were two girls with long, strawberry blonde hair who looked much older than me, more developed on top, and taller by several inches. They wore tight blue jeans, t-shirts, and sneakers. Behind them was a boy, taller than me, with rippling muscles in his arms, legs, and chest, a flat belly, with a square face and chin, and short, sandy colored hair. I was staring at him, my mind sending strange signals to my belly and nether regions, when Pa walked up behind me, smacking me a stinging blow across the back of the head.

"Quit gawking at that boy, and get back to work, bitch. Unless you want a beating you won't soon forget."

"No, sir. I mean yes, sir." I resumed mowing the lawn.

Pa went inside, and I stole furtive glances at the boy. Every time I looked at him my belly filled with butterflies and I felt the need to pee. It was a giddy sensation, like riding a roller coaster.

When I looked away my body settled down until I looked at him again.

Within days of their arrival, the man and the boy were installing a porch swing. The day after that the boy was preparing a garden in their back yard. The muscles of his body pressed against the tight material of his shorts and t-shirt. I was raking the yard as the boy and his father repainted their back porch and did other minor repairs. Every morning at seven, the boy stood in the back yard, in skin-tight spandex shorts and no shirt, performing graceful movements that looked like a dance involving punching and kicking.

One day, a few weeks after they moved in, I was in the front yard raking up grass cuttings. He waved at me from the porch swing and I waved back. My stomach rose toward my throat as he stood up and walked toward my house. He was dressed in a grey porkpie hat, jeans, a grey t-shirt, and shiny black loafers. I was focusing on raking so that he wouldn't see how nervous I was. Pa must have seen him, too, because he stepped onto the porch as the boy approached. Pa walked into the yard, grabbed me by the arm with a numbing grip, and pushed me toward the house.

The next day, after Pa left for work, the doorbell rang. I was washing the dishes, so Ma answered the door.

"May I help you?" Ma's voice was friendly but strained.

"Hi. My name is Vinnie Il-Cazzo. We moved in down the block a couple weeks back. I saw your daughter in the yard yesterday, and thought I would introduce myself." The voice was a baritone and sent delightful shivers down my spine.

"Which daughter? Stephanie Ann is your age, and Caroline June is a bit younger. My name is Heather Baker, by the way." Ma sounded as nervous as I felt.

"Pleased to meet you, Mrs Baker. I'm thinking it has to be Stephanie Ann. She has long red hair and bangs. She's a bit shorter than me."

"That would be Stephanie Ann, alright." Ma gave a curt laugh. "Well, I suppose you could introduce yourself, but we don't socialize with our neighbors much. Myron prefers that we tend to our own. He's my husband."

"I think I saw him. He pulled Stephanie Ann inside before I could come over."

Caroline and I walked to the doorway, and stood next to Ma. I blushed and twisted my toe into the floor. "Hi. I'm Steph. This is my sister Caroline. Sorry about yesterday. I saw you coming over but..."

"It was time to eat. Myron likes us all at the table." Ma interrupted me.

Caroline nodded and walked back into the house with Ma. I stepped out onto the porch.

Vinnie dressed finer than any boy in the neighborhood. I remember that being my first impression.

"How do?" He tipped his hat and nodded his head in an abbreviated bow. "Vincenzo Cassiel Michelangelo Il-Cazzo is what they tagged me with, but cats call me Vinnie. Some call me Il-Cazzo." He winked, and I felt a sudden moisture down below.

"Hi. Nice to meet you, Vinnie. I'm sorry about yesterday but...yeah we were having lunch. Ummm, meatloaf and potatoes." Pa had us well trained to make excuses that ended conversation from strangers.

"Savvy. I wanted to introduce myself. You're definitely all that, and I was hoping we could get acquainted." He blushed and looked away.

"Thank you. I don't have many boys saying that. I'm not that popular. I'd like to be friends, but Caroline and I don't get to play much. When I'm doing yard chores Pa expects me to focus on them. By the way, I better get back to the breakfast dishes." I scanned the street in case Pa returned for some reason.

The following week Vinnie approached Pa while I was vacuuming. I couldn't hear what they said, but that Sunday Pa said that we were giving Vinnie a ride to church.

"You girls just keep your mouths shut and your eyes off of him. Don't start getting friendly, or I swear you'll regret it."

"Oh my, Steph's boyfriend is coming to church." Caroline giggled.

Pa slapped her across the face and she started sobbing. "Cut the tears, or I'll give you something to cry about!"

Caroline ran to the bathroom, and when she came out she stared straight ahead while drying the dinner dishes.

Vinnie appeared on Sunday as we were leaving the house. He was dressed in a grey pinstripe suit, a black tuxedo shirt, and a white tie. He had a grey fedora on his head, and smelled of an enticing aftershave.

Pa glared at him. "Hey, boy, didn't know if you were coming or not. Next time don't cut it so close."

"Yes, sir." Vinnie stared at him with a look that showed no fear. I had never seen anyone look at Pa that way.

I was dressed in a peach dress that came to my knees, white tights and pink shoes. I had been up late listening to Pa laying into Caroline for not cleaning the water off the floor after her bath. Her sobs and his yelling made me sick to my stomach, but self-preservation kept me in bed.

I gave Vinnie a half-smile as I climbed in the back seat with Ma and Caroline. They were dressed in matching violet dresses with black pumps. We remained quiet. Caroline grimaced as she sat on her welted bottom.

Pa, dressed in a black suit, white shirt and yellow tie, pulled off in the truck. He looked at Vinnie. "Want a cup of joe, boy?"

I gulped. Pa put whiskey in his coffee. I said nothing, but Ma wasn't so smart. She leaned forward. "Myron, honey, his parents might not like him drinking coffee."

Pa gave her a look through the rearview mirror and she shrunk back. "I wasn't asking you, dear." He pulled a styrofoam cup from the glove compartment. "Pour yourself some, boy. It'll put hair on your ass."

I blushed as my mind decided to wonder if Vinnie had hair down there. I was starting to, and assumed he did too. I tried thinking about something else.

Vinnie poured a cup of coffee, took a sip, and gasped. He smiled and nodded,

"Appreciate it, sir. Better than the stuff I

make."

"I reckon. Must be my secret ingredient." Pa laughed.

Vinnie didn't react negatively to drinking from which I assumed that he drank, or had before. That wasn't a point in his favor. I had enough to deal with when Pa drank -- which was all the time. Vinnie was handsome and turned my insides to jelly, but the idea that he liked alcohol terrified me.

A half hour later we pulled up in front of the church. As I was climbing out of the truck, I noticed Vinnie staring at Caroline where a dark red mark showed below the hem of her dress. My stomach knotted into a ball. I prayed that he would keep his mouth shut. Pa wouldn't say anything, but later Caroline, Ma, and I would pay dearly.

Ma took Caroline and me to the ladies room as Vinnie signed the visitors book. After we were seated in the pews, Caroline and I shifted a bit trying to get comfortable.

Pa glared. "You two planing to sit still, or do we need to have a chat in the parking lot?"

The shifting stopped. Even so, there was a better than average chance that a strap was in our near future. It didn't take much.

After the choir performed several numbers, Pastor Pehr Gaphals began preaching his sermon. It was on the dangers of drinking. It was Pa's turn to shift in his seat, his fingers drumming on his thighs. Ma tried holding his hands, and his eyes smoldered. Ma was in for a beating later, too.

Fifteen minutes into the sermon, Pa excused himself to go use the men's room. Vinniestared straight ahead while writing something on a napkin. He slipped it to me, and I read it.

This is my cell number. If you need help or they do, call or text. Memorize and destroy.

I shoved the napkin inside my pocket, and sat listening without moving. Vinnie had a strong body, he worked out in his yard, but he wasn't in Pa's league. I prayed that he would stay out of my problems. I didn't want Pa to kill him.

Pa returned twenty minutes later. The sermon ended, and the pastor's wife announced a potluck two weeks away and a class on baptism. We filed out and Pa drove us home. He drummed his fingers on the steering wheel, his mouth a thin hard line. I knew that he was in a rage over the sermon.

For two weeks the bruises on my butt and lower back healed. Pa had taken his rage out on me and Caroline. Whatever we did for the three days after church wasn't good enough, or done fast enough. I watched Vinnie working out in his backyard every day and considered calling his cell number. I was afraid to let him know what was happening. Pa owned several guns, and, as I mentioned, he wouldn't have hesitated to kill Vinnie if Vinnie attacked him. I suspected that if Vinnie knew the truth, he would interfere. I was correct.

Two weeks after the sermon on drinking, Pa parked our truck at church. Across the parking lot, the Il-Cazzo's were climbing out of a minivan. Vinnie's father moved at an angle and cornered Pa. His mother turned and greeted Ma. While Ma and Pa were being kept busy, Vinnie and his sister approached me and Caroline.

"Hi. We don't get much chance to visit, even though we're neighbors and all. My name's Tori." Vinnie's sister gushed. "Vinnie tells me that you're Steph, and this is Caroline?"

I nodded and twisted the toe of my shoe into the ground. Out of the corner of my eye I noticed Pa looking pissed, but he couldn't get around Vinnie's father.

Tori gave Pa a disgusted look, and then looked at Ma with an evil eye. In a loud voice she asked, "Caroline? What happened to your eye? It's red and puffy. You OK? Looks like you went a few rounds with someone."

"I fell. Uh, I was getting up after dinner

and I tripped and bumped a chair." Caroline turned away.

"Really? That sucks!" Vinnie glared at Pa with open menace. "Glad you didn't fall too, Steph. I guess you must have a couple weeks ago when you had that nasty bruise on your thigh. Maybe I should teach you both some martial arts to improve your balance."

Pa pushed Vinnie's father aside with a snarl and grabbed Ma by the shoulder. He looked at me and Caroline, and we fell in behind him. The Il-Cazzo's seated themselves three rows behind us.

After church Pa drove us home without staying for the potluck. He didn't say a word about what happened before church, and once we got inside the house, he grabbed a six pack of beer from the fridge and turned on a baseball game. Caroline and I got busy shelling peas for dinner, and Ma started preparing a chicken.

After ninety minutes, the six pack was finished. Pa roared at me, "Hey! Stephanie! Get your ass over here with another beer!"

I jumped up and dashed into the kitchen. Ma handed me a can of beer and I hurried back to Pa. In my haste I spilled a little of the beer.

"You clumsy little bitch! When I tell one of you kids to do something, you better do it right!"

Pa jumped to his feet and grabbed me with a powerful left hand. Beer flew in one direction, my head rocking in the other, as he backhanded me across the face with a vicious right hand. The salty taste of blood filled my mouth, and my lower lip swelled. Pa threw me onto the floor, yanked me back up, and herded me down the hall with repeated slaps to my butt. He shoved me into his and Ma's bedroom, and pushed me face down over the king sized bed. In his drunken rage he reached to the wall and took down one of his belts from a hook. I tried moving away, but Pa pinned me to the bed with his left hand. Holding the doubled over strap in his right hand he began to mercilessly whip me. I screamed, but that enraged him further.

"I fucking provide for you kids and your drunken bitch of a mother! I work hard! So when I say get me a fucking beer, you fucking better get it! And don't spill it! You do as I tell you or so help me! You got that you little bitch? Why couldn't you have been a boy? Daughters are fucking useless!"

Pa punctuated his curses and rants with stripes from the belt. He yanked down my shorts as I lay limp, sobbing and pleading. My voice was all but gone from the strain of screaming.

"I'm sorry! I'll be careful! Please stop! Don't whip me anymore! Please stop, please!

I'll be good! I'll be careful! Please!" I rasped.

It was to no avail, as the belt landed on my naked flesh. I shrieked, and Ma dashed into the room. "Stop it Myron! Stop beating that child I said! She's had enough." She grabbed Pa's arm.

Pa turned, and wordlessly, with muscle knotted arms, knocked Ma into the door jamb where she crumpled. Pa tossed the belt onto the bed and looked down at us.

"I'm going over to the Red Hen to have me a whiskey and see the guys. When I get home there best be dinner on the table, and these brats had best be acting right. You got that, bitch?"

He stormed out of the room, down the hall, slamming the front door behind him. The sound of his truck roaring to life and pulling away drifted through the bedroom window. Ma stood up and almost fell again. She hobbled over to the bed to comfort me. I looked up, making a fateful decision I've never entirely regretted.

"There's a number, you got to call it," I whispered with a croak. "Call Vinnie. Get help."

Ma grabbed the cell phone and dialed.

"Hello? Yes, Vinnie? I need your parents. Yes, we're in danger, young man." A pause. "Yes, Antoinette? It's Heather Baker. We need help." She listened for a minute and then ended the call.

Ma walked to the kitchen as Caroline sat against the wall with her arms wrapped around me. I had no tears left, but she was whimpering. Ma returned with four garbage bags. "Girls. Don't ask questions. Get your clothes, stuffed animals, books, anything important, and put it in these bags. Vinnie and his Pa are on their way."

Sure enough, while we were packing, there was a knock on the door. I peeked around the corner and Vinnie's father came through the door fast. He had a pistol in his hand and turned each direction checking the room. "We're clear, son! Move it. Help the girls pack and get the items into the van."

Vinnie stepped through the door, dressed in loose shorts, a tank top, and leather boots. He crabbed sideways with his hands raised to his chest in fists. His father stepped outside and returned with their minivan.

Vinnie walked over and hugged Ma without a sound. She tried to smile, and then pointed toward us. Vinnie turned and the look in his eyes scared me. He took several deep breaths. "You just sealed your fate, you bastard!"

He muttered.

Vinnie's eyes softened, and he helped me stand up. Caroline moved to start packing. Vinnie looked into my eyes. "Hey, hey Steph. Caroline. You're safe now. Papa's getting the van and stuff. We're going to help you. What happened?" The hurt in his voice came through his attempts to sound calm.

I hugged Vinnie around the chest and buried my face in his tank-top. He smelled of sweat and cologne, rugged and virile. "We got home from church. Pa was in a mood. He didn't like what you and your sister said at church." I rasped.

We joined Caroline in our room and packed all our clothes, stuffed animals, and books. I pulled out ten dollars from my piggy bank. As we took the bags to the hall Vinnie scooped Caroline off the floor and gave her a reassuring hug. "This ends here, kid. You're safe."

After setting Caroline down, Vinnie turned toward me. We hugged, and I buried my face in his chest again. Something stirred deep inside my belly and just below. My bottom and legs were on fire from the belt, my throat was raw from screaming, and my eyes were swollen from crying -- my mouth was sore from where it had split open when Pa slapped me -- but mixed with the agony, and terror, was an entirely new sensation.

Vinnie tilted my face up with a soft hand under my chin, and gave me a kiss. Not a kiss like Ma gave, or my relatives gave, this was harder, feral, and full on my mouth. I returned it with equal force. There was a strange feeling down below, and it made all the physical pain less. We stopped kissing as quickly as we had started, and carried the bags to the front door.

Mr. Il-Cazzo parked the minivan on the side street, climbed out, and tossed Vinnie a bundle of clothes. Vinnie walked back to Caroline's and my bedroom, and without a blush undressed. I stared at him in his socks and jockey shorts. He was hard and solid from his shoulders to his ankles, his skin pale where the tan lines ended. There was a noticeable bulge in the front of his undershorts that made my heart thump faster. He put on black jeans, a grey t-shirt, placed his wallet in his right pocket, a short steel cylinder in a pocket on his right thigh, and a thick billfold into his left pocket. As he tied his boots, I knelt down and hugged him again. "Thank you. Thank you."

We loaded the van with bags of clothes and personal items. Vinnie placed three pillows on a seat for me. I gave one of them to Caroline, and sat in the other two. It hurt to sit, even so.

Vinnie climbed in the back of the van behind me and Caroline, and Ma and his father sat up front.

As Vinnie repacked the garbage bags into suitcases, Ma filled in Vinnie's father on what had transpired. "When we got home from church, Myron went to the living room to watch a baseball game on TV and drink his beer. The girls and I started supper going and tried to remain quiet. He was pissed that your daughter and Vinnie called him out for slapping Caroline. It seems like every day one of the girls manages to set him off, or I do. He gets provoked, then he slaps us or beats one of the girls. I've never been able to break free. I've got nowhere to turn." Ma's voice was soft and strained. She held her head in her hands.

Vinnie finished the repacking and climbed into the seat between me and Caroline. I leaned against his shoulder saying nothing. Vinnie held me close, his hand stroking between my thighs, and listened to Ma.

"Myron was finished with his first six pack. It's our life. Myron watches sports and gets drunk when he isn't at the lot running the car compactor. I don't like his behavior, but I'm scared. I mean, where the hell can I go? Who would want me?"

Vinnie's eyes narrowed as he drew me and Caroline closer and hugged us. Caroline was looking over her shoulder and whimpering. I closed my eyes and pressed my face into Vinnie. There was a strong spicy aroma of cologne emanating from his face. I felt safe for the moment.

Ma continued recounting the events.

When she finished, Vinnie's father patted her on the shoulder. "It's going to be all right. This ends here and now." He sounded eerily calm. It was as terrifying as the fire in Vinnie's eyes. I knew we were safe, but the anger that radiated from Vinnie and his father made me shudder.

Ma groaned. "I finally reached my breaking point. I tried to restrain Myron's arm. He turned and knocked me into the door. Then he said he was going over to the Red Hen to have some whiskey and see the guys. He ordered us to clean the house and make dinner. After he left, Stephanie told me to call you, and I did." Heather held her forehead. "I'm having trouble seeing clearly. Everything wants to split in two. Where are you taking us?"

"A place I heard about. They can stash you for a few days until we handle this. Then you have to keep going. Believe me that this isn't going to end well. You can't go back." We cruised down the street of a neighboring town.

The place was hardscrabble and decrepit.

I leaned up and kissed Vinnie on the cheek. He turned his head and kissed me on the lips. I blushed. "Thank you for coming! Thank you!" My voice was a frog croak.

"I'd come for you any time, doll." He stroked my face with his fingers.

Vinnie's father turned on the radio, pressed a button, and Pink Floyd's "Don't Leave Me Now" filled the car.

Ma sat holding her head and looking pale. "Stand" by Poison crackled through the speakers. That was followed by "In My Time of Dying" by Led Zeppelin. An hour later Vinnie's father pulled off at an exit and drove us past a sign that read "Welcome to Pardmest."

The town of Pardmest is nothing but a strip mall, a gas station, a feed store and an adult store. We stopped at the strip mall, and Vinnie ran inside of a burger chain. He returned with five double cheeseburger meals, and chocolate milkshakes. We ate in silence while "Crazy Diamond" by Pink Floyd filled the car.

On the edge of Pardmest sat an old, three story, victorian style house that had once been a motel. The motel had gone out of business instead of competing with the cluster of economy chains five miles to the south. An organization dedicated to assisting abused women and children like us purchased the hotel building for use as a shelter. There was a garage below the first floor large enough to accommodate fifteen vehicles. Vinnie's father pulled up to the front of the shelter at high speed and slammed on the brakes.

"Stay put, son. Watch the girls. I need to arrange for them to stay here. At least for tonight."

As his father climbed out of the van and approached the building Caroline leaned across Vinnie and whispered. "You OK, Steph?" She gave me a sympathetic look.

"My butt and my legs are on fire and it hurts to move. I'm scared. What are we going to do now?" I whispered back.

"I don't know. We have to take care of each other I guess. Like the time when Pa left for three days after he and Ma had that fight. Remember how Ma had to go to the hospital and told us not to tell anyone? And, when she came home she was in bed all day? We took care of each other then and we will now. But now we also have Vinnie and his Pa." Caroline tried to sound brave but she began to cry. Vinnie drew us into a hug.

"I'll take care of you like I always do. You have to be brave, OK? You just have to be." I rasped, brushing the tears from Caroline's eyes with caressing fingers.

"Hey! If my father says you're going to be safe, then you can wrap your ass in a sling and bet it." Vinnie kissed Caroline on the forehead and me on the lips. "So help me, if your dirtbag father comes looking around, I have a mind to take him jitterbugging at knuckle junction. He might be flushed out in the strength department, but if you take the tallest guy in the world and shatter his knee, that's a universal equalizer. Then it's a simple side kick to the face. End of story." Vinnie hugged us closer.

Ma and Vinnie's father approached the house and knocked on the door. A woman answered. She was a bit shy of six foot with short cropped auburn hair and the shoulders and chest of a weightlifter. Dressed bottom to top in biker boots, jeans and a sleeveless flannel shirt she was intimidating. The lady eyeballed Ma, said something and then glanced beyond her at the van.

Vinnie's father and the lady were talking when, in a moment of inglorious agony, Ma barfed on the floor of the porch and collapsed in a crumpled heap. Vinnie grabbed Caroline to keep her from jumping out of the van. "Both of you grab some seat cushion. Please. We make like statues until they come to get us."

"Oh holy Hell! Roz! Come quick. Bring Becca with you." The burly woman shouted into the door of the shelter loud enough for us to hear her.

A woman, my height, but built of solid muscle, came running. She had medium length, spiky blonde hair, a ruddy complexion, and intense eyes. On her heels was a girl barely out of high school. The girl had straight, raven black hair to her shoulders and dark piercing eyes. Her skin was milky white in contrast to her hair. Seeing Ma collapsed in a pool of vomit, and taking notice of the three of us in the van, the eighteen year old, Becca Dunwoody, ran to us. She noted that the keys were in the ignition. Becca climbed into the driver's seat and spoke over her shoulder to us. "Hold on tight, we're going in."

She turned the key and the motor roared to life. Pulling a remote from her pocket and pressing a button, she waited for the garage door to open, pulled forward and parked sideways. Hopping out and pocketing the keys she opened the rear door and we climbed out.

Up a flight of stairs, we entered a living room the size of a hotel lobby. Roz was setting Ma down on a couch, checking her pulse, and breathing. Ma was breathing normally but was unresponsive. "Looks like a concussion. She needs medical attention, Pat. I can call Otis. He's got corpsman training. If anything needs to happen beyond his skills, he can call it in without involving us."

"I've had first aid training as well as survival training as a young man." Vinnie's father stated. "Why don't you get the kids settled somewhere and let me take a look at Heather."

Becca led Vinnie, Caroline, and me up a long staircase and into a bedroom with two double beds. The lady called Pat followed us, and Becca looked back at her.

"Any chance of getting these kids some food, or ice cream, while we talk?"

My eyes lit up as did Caroline's. Not much bad could happen that ice cream wouldn't excite a kid.

Pat headed downstairs and returned with three plates of roast beef sandwiches and chips. Placing the tray of plates on a side table, with cans of Dr Pepper, she told us, "you kids can eat as much as you like. If you want more let Becca know. I need to go tend to your mother, but my friend here will keep you company."

Caroline and I were eating, when someone knocked a 1-3-2 pattern from downstairs. I tensed up, setting my plate on the side table, as Vinnie slid out the door smooth and silent. Caroline and I looked at each other. Becca gave a reassuring smile.

"It's OK. That's a friend who came to check on your mom. The knock is our signal."

Caroline and I resumed eating until Vinnie stepped back into the bedroom. I finished and lay on my belly on a bed. Sitting hurt too much. Caroline was was sitting far back on the other bed hugging her knees.

Vinnie sat beside me, rubbing my shoulders. "It's copacetic, chicks. There's a regular bull of a guy down there. I could take him if needs be, but he looks to be friend not foe."

I looked at Vinnie and my tears started again. The adrenaline was wearing off, and fear gripped me. Something about the way Vinnie was reacting simultaneously scared and aroused me. I readjusted my position and put my head in his lap. Becca sat holding Caroline's hand.

"I need to know what happened. I can't help unless I know." Becca frowned.

As nice as the people were, I wasn't ready to trust them. Not yet. "You can't help anyway. No one can. Pa told me to do something and I didn't do it immediately. He had to give me a whipping. Ma came in and told him to stop, and he pushed her away. She tripped on something, and fell in the doorway. It was an accident."

Becca gave me sympathetic eyes. "Do these accidents happen often? What could be so important for you to do that you deserve to be whipped for it?"

I glanced at Caroline who returned the look. "Ma's clumsy sometimes. We are too. I try to be good, but Pa told me to do a chore and I didn't get right on it. Children have to obey their parents. It's in the Bible."

Becca nodded. "It's important to tell us the truth about what happened. We need to know because your mother might get sicker if we don't treat her properly."

I scowled as mean as I could. "I'm not lying! I have to protect Ma and Caroline. I told you the truth. I'm not letting us get sent away to some home for bad kids. Not going to happen!"

Vinnie shook his head. "Steph? Caroline? Do you trust me? Do you trust my father?" He stroked my hair. "I dig that you don't know us enough for full trust, but I've been playing every angle all summer to spend time with you. I heard what your mother said went down. I swear I'll protect you both. With my life if it comes to that. You've seen me in my backyard this summer working out in the early bright. Have no doubts that I can keep you safe. Your father is only human, and humans rely on their knees to stand. Next time I see him his knees won't work, if you dig the riff. The son of a bitch is going to have problems his cranium can't tolerate, you dig? So please tell Miss Becca what she wants to know."

I stared at Vinnie, my heart thumping harder. Things I didn't dare dream of doing, but wanted to, he was offering to do. I wrapped my arms around his strong waist. Caroline started crying and the poured out the entire story. I added details where needed, because it hurt to talk.

Becca reached out and stroked my head and then Caroline's. I flinched. Becca sighed, "I've lived through similar events. My mom was an alcoholic and my dad too. I had to get help when I was fifteen because they were always beating on me. I never told Pat and Roz for a month about them drinking. See, they said if I told I would be sent to juvenile hall or a group home and get nasty things done to me."

I looked up, shocked that someone understood. "Yeah. I know. I'm never going to those places and neither is sissy. Anyone tries that and..." I slammed a fist on the side table and rattled the dishes.

Vinnie's eyes widened, his eyebrows moved up his forehead, and the corners of his mouth turned up. He helped me sit up on a pillow, and held me in his arms with my face on his powerful chest. Vinnie ran a hand over my back and behind but stopped when I flinched in pain. I felt his reaction to my body pressed against his. In spite of the pain, I was reacting too.

There was a knock on the door, and Vinnie's sister Tori walked in with one of the scariest men I'd ever encountered. Scarier, even, than Pa. Vinnie introduced the man as Otis LeMar. Otis was six and a half feet tall, built like a brick wall, and had reddish-bronze skin. His black hair hung down the back of his head in a braid. He wore tennis shoes, cargo pants and a combat vest over a muscled and bulging bare chest. His arms were built like two cannons and his hands like anvils. I gripped Vinnie for all I was worth.

Tori surveyed the room. "This gentleman needs to talk to Steph and Caroline. Papa's downstairs with their mother. Mama's in the kitchen with two of the ladies who run this place. You and I need to talk, bro." Tori helped me stand up and move over to where Caroline was sitting.

Otis turned toward Vinnie with a stern glare. "Hey! What's your name?"

"Vinnie. Be careful with them. They're real fragile, and I'm real protective."

"Yeah, right. I saw what you were starting to do downstairs. I don't know where you trained, but you have good moves and good instincts. We should talk later." Otis put out a hand and they shook.

Otis looked at me and Caroline as he squatted by the bed. "I have some herbs boiling on the stove downstairs. Mrs. Il-Cazzo is going to come up in a few minutes with a poultice. Stephanie is it? You need to put it on your buttocks and thighs," Otis took a breath. "Girls your mother is quite sick. She has a concussion from hitting her head. Her brain literally slammed to one side of her skull on impact with something heavy and solid. Then it ricocheted back to slam the other side of her skull. She will get sicker before she gets well. I can treat her now, and other people can continue to do so, but I must know how this happened. The truth.

Caroline looked confused. "We know she's sick. Why does everyone keep calling us liars?" Her voice turned defiant. "Fine. Pa drinks a lot. He gets angry a lot. We don't talk about that, see? We aren't supposed to ever talk about it. Not ever. Yes, he whipped sissy. He shoved Ma so hard she hit her head on the doorway. If you tell anyone I said so, I will have our friend Vinnie bash your head in like Pa said he would do to me if I ever talked out of turn. You got that? I will tell him to kill you!"

Vinnie and Tori froze, staring at us.

Becca backed off several steps. I grabbed

Caroline and pulled her away, scared, waiting for Otis to hit one of us.

Otis looked down at us. "Yes ma'am, I hear you. I don't need to tell anyone else. I got this. So, If anyone tries to hurt you, your sister, or your mother ever again I will personally cripple them for life. You best believe."

I looked up at him and nodded. He was clearly serious. He cared. I had no idea why, but he cared. "Good. We understand each other. Sorry that my sister threatened you. I'll talk with her about it later."

"No need. She's in defensive mode, and that's good." Otis left the room. Vinnie and Tori followed him.

Vinnie returned upstairs twenty minutes later with three bowls of vanilla ice cream. Caroline had changed into her nightgown and I was in a long t-shirt on my belly with a flannel poultice on my flanks. Vinnie served the ice cream, and climbed onto the bed I was in. We ate, and soon after were holding each other in a warm, soft embrace. I relaxed as Becca turned on the radio in the background and took the empty dishes before leaving the room.

"What is this music? I've never heard it before." I rasped and yawned.

Vinnie kissed me on the cheek. "Mahler's Kindertotenlieder."

As Caroline began to breathe more deeply in sleep, I snuggled in with my body pressed against Vinnie.

2

Vinnie woke up moments before true dawn. One minute I was warm and comfy, breathing in his scent, the next there was an empty void. I lay under the sheets in my panties, having pulled off my t-shirt after a while. The poultice had helped, but my butt and legs were still sore. Caroline was in the other bed in her nightgown engaged in soft somniloquy. Vinnie and I had slept the whole night together with him holding me. There was plenty of kissing and cuddling, nothing more than that, but once I fell asleep I had strange dreams. Vinnie and me on a beach blanket doing things I'd only ever read about. I blushed thinking about it.

Vinnie slid out of bed in his jockey shorts, looking uncomfortable and walking strangely. He checked the doors, found the bathroom, and the sound of water filled the room. I giggled to myself at the thought of joining him. I'd seen it in a movie before. A half hour later I was dozing when Vinnie emerged dressed in his clothes from the day before. A light knock on the door startled me.

Vinnie stepped back, and to the side, before flinging the door open. It was Tori. "Vinnie?" She whispered. "I heard the shower running from next door. There's a bathroom in each room, I guess. Anyway, I brought you your knapsack last night with as many clothes as I could fit in it. I forgot to give it to you."

Vinnie grabbed his sack. "Thanks, gate. Wasn't sure what to do. I need fresh threads."

Caroline was asleep, and I guess Vinnie thought I was. He set a clean outfit on the chair and undressed. I had never seen a naked male except in magazines, and Vinnie was. I didn't know what he'd done with his jockey shorts, but he wasn't wearing them under his jeans. I bit my lip so I wouldn't gasp as he pulled on fresh clothes. The sight of him without clothes set off feelings I couldn't explain. He was better looking than any magazine picture, that was for certain. I let a giggle escape as he dressed, and he turned and winked at me.

"I thought you were both asleep, else I would have changed in the bathroom."

I grinned and nodded. He chuckled and kissed me on the lips while stroking my face.

"You should go have a bath and get dressed," he traced a finger over my freckled tummy and up to my small, blossoming chest.

I sat up gingerly and winced, before walking to the bathroom with some clean clothes. I scrubbed as best I could, crying as the water hit my bruises. An hour later, as the sun was creeping out, Caroline awoke. A half hour later she emerged from her bath, and the three of us crept downstairs.

We entered the kitchen where Vinnie's parents and the three ladies who ran the shelter were all sitting drinking coffee. Tori was in the living room with Ma and Otis LeMar. Vinnie gave his mother a kiss on the cheek and hugged his father.

"Morning, gates. Let's percolate. I'd have come down sooner but the ladies needed to freshen up first." Vinnie winked at his father who laughed.

Pat and Roz stood, poured orange juice, and started making bacon and scrambled eggs. "That's fine. We usually bring breakfast to the rooms." Becca yawned. "Did you sleep all right?"

"It was very nice. The bed I mean." I blushed and hid my face in my hands.

Vinnie's father gave him a look with his head tilted. "I'm glad you slept well, Steph."

"I slept quite well. So, when do we light out? I'm ready for anything." Vinnie shrugged at his father.

"You generally are, Vinnie my lad." His father gave him stern eyes. "First you kids need to get your feed on. Then I want you girls to sit with your mother while Vinnie helps carry food to the various rooms with Ms. Dunwoody." He motioned to Becca. "Unless anything changes, we'll leave after lunch."

Roz brought us each a plate piled with sliced melon, eggs, bacon, and toast. Tori entered and was likewise served. I ate and had a heaping plate of seconds.

Vinnie sipped a cup of coffee. "Tori? Did you by chance grab my envelopes and stuff from my top dresser drawer?"

"I did. Your laptop and iPod, too. I wasn't sure what books to bring but I think we can grab any of that on the road." Tori smiled. "Oh, and later on I have a gift for you from Fisher as well."

After we finished eating, Tori sat and made small talk with me and Caroline while Vinnie carried trays of food upstairs.

I was nibbling more toast when a loud banging on the front door split the air. Otis came through the kitchen door quickly.

"Upstairs. The five-oh just arrived." Otis, Tori, and Mrs. Il-Cazzo motioned us to move. Ma propped herself on the shoulder of Vinnie's mother. We slipped into a bedroom and shut the door.

I tiptoed into a bathroom with a hand over my mouth and lost much of my breakfast leaning over the toilet. Caroline sat against a wall, knees to her chest, convulsing, as silent tears fell. Ma sat on the bed leaning on Mrs. Il-Cazzo. Otis stood by the door, and I noticed he held a pistol in his hand. I hadn't seen one earlier. Tori helped me clean my face, and hugged me.

"If it's him, get your mama and Caroline into the bathroom, and lock the door. Only open it if you hear me say "The rat is in the trap.""

I nodded. "What are you going to do?"

"If it's your papa, I'm going to make him my bitch. He'll wish he'd never been born." Tori had the same fire in her eyes that Vinnie had. The Il-Cazzo's were frightening, and something about their presence made me feel braver. Like owning a large guard dog that you're not sure you can control, but that you know is loyal.

Twenty minutes later Vinnie gave the one-three-two knock. Otis let him in, and Vinnie helped to carry our suitcases downstairs. He loaded them into the back of the minivan. Ma climbed into the back seat and Otis sat beside her. Tori sat on the other side. Mrs. Il-Cazzo climbed behind the wheel with Mr. Il-Cazzo riding shotgun. Vinnie, Caroline, and I snuggled together in the far back with the luggage surrounding us. Vinnie had his right hand just below my belly, stroking me. Caroline was on my other side and I held her close.

Otis made a phone call to some friends and the van was presently surrounded by three slow moving farm vehicles. The police behind us lost sight of the van as Vinnie's mother pulled onto the freeway.

Forty minutes later Tori called out "Allez Allez Oxen Free!" Vinnie, Caroline, and I climbed into the rear-most seats and buckled up. We drove west for an hour and then stopped to rearrange the seating. Vinnie and his father switched the license plates. There were extra plates from Arkansas under the floor mat of the passenger seat. Two hours after that, Vinnie's father pulled off at an exit and drove us on a two-lane road lined on both sides with places that looked seedy. There were strips of pawn shops, off-brand fast food emporiums, used car dealerships, dollar stores, and no contract cell phone dealers. Bars and adult entertainment venues were crammed between the stores. A few miles ahead the businesses thinned out in favor of some empty looking trailer courts and abandoned building lots. We stopped and Otis took the wheel. He drove for another half mile until, to one side, I saw lights strung through the trees and a clearing in the woods.

The clearing had a derelict shack in the

center and tables and chairs set around it in the gravel and dirt. The shack had a chimney which was belching smoke and heat. The smell of slow-cooked meat wafted through the air.

"OK with everyone?" Otis inquired.

"Looks fine to me. Smells delicious." Mrs. Il-Cazzo sounded cheerful.

"Good for us, too" Ma murmured. She had an ice pack on her forehead.

Once Otis parked, Vinnie stepped out with his father and scouted the surroundings. He nodded to his father, and gave us the all clear sign. Tori helped Ma out of the van. Caroline and I climbed out, and Mrs. Il-Cazzo hugged us. Otis had a stretch, and cracked his joints.

The barbecue place had no name and no actual menu. There was a choice of meat, with slaw and either white bread or baked beans on the side, and three different kinds of canned soda-pop. Styrofoam plates, plastic forks, paper napkins, cash only, and our waitress was a pre-pubescent girl with braids sticking out every which way and a disarming grin. Otis had been there before, and said that he was planning to part company with us after lunch. He knew someone who would give him a ride back to Pardmest.

We each ordered a half rack of ribs. Tori and Vinnie chose the beans, as did their parents and Otis. Caroline, Ma, and I opted for bread. We all had Dr. Pepper. The air was warm and the food was tasty. We ate slowly, but Vinnie kept looking around, and stiffening when new cars pulled up.

"Steph, what's your favorite subject in school?" Otis asked

"I like English and science." My voice was improving, but still hoarse.

"I like reading and music class," Caroline took a large gulp of Dr. Pepper.

"Always liked reading, myself. Never cared for science until later in life. I think it's good that you enjoy school. It helps later on." Otis was looking everywhere and nowhere at once.

"You sound like you didn't like school." Ma frowned while sucking a bone.

"Didn't like it?" Otis cocked his head to the side and made a face. "I loathed it. To be fair it wasn't the education that bothered me. The teachers had big mouths, and they reported a lot of crap to my pops. I always felt like I was in his way, and then if they reported some imagined or wholly fabricated wrong I'd committed, it caused more issues. He always believed the teachers, and after browbeating me, I would say that yeah I had done whatever. Rarely had I done a damned thing. I suspect that my teachers looked for excuses to be jerks because they had unhappy lives. They knew my pops would believe them so I was a good target. I've always thought he was irritated by life, and he used those reports as an excuse to get pissed at me. Big reason why I skeined out at seventeen and joined the navy."

Ma shuddered. "I've known people like your Pa. One of the reasons I left home and got involved with Myron was to escape parents like that."

I listened, more alert now. Ma had never talked about herself, and I was interested. Caroline sat shifting around, trying not to interrupt. Vinnie excused himself, and escorted her to the facilities.

"How did you ever get involved with a bastard like that?" Mrs. Il-Cazzo picked some rib meat from her teeth,

Ma drew me close, looking at some arbitrary point in the distance. "Damned if I know why I stayed so long, but in the beginning, well, it was different. I was born to a strict family in the northern plains states. Church, and a lot of it, was the lynchpin of the week. I was treated like a less than because I had questions about most everything others held as articles of faith. Plus, my parents were overbearing. They insisted on knowing everything I was doing, and were forever talking to my teachers at school, the leaders at church, and pumping my few friends for information about me. I wanted to live my life my own way. One day this tall, rugged, and muscular hunk of virility started hanging around. Myron was a truck driver, and he was five years older than me. I started finding reasons to go to the library every day so we could make out in the stacks. I invited him to church, and he accepted. He showed up most days after school to offer me a ride." Ma smiled with a faraway look in her eyes. "When I turned eighteen, and graduated high school, my life became my own. My folks never approved, but it wasn't their choice. Myron promised he'd settle down at a steady job, and send me to college. We moved to Harvest Junction, and he did take a steady job compacting junked cars. The college never materialized, because inside of three months I was in the family way. Steph came along, and soon after Myron started spending more and more time at the local bar. He was short tempered and expected me to tend to the baby. I'd been raised to believe that was a woman's duty. We fought a lot over his drinking, and many was the time he slapped me around or hit me with a belt. Once or twice he punched me. I figured it was my consequence for rebelliousness as a child. Then one day he changed. Steph was two and not crying as much. He worked a lot of over-time. It was like he became the sweet man I loved again. He stopped drinking and life was good. We still weren't very social with the neighbors, but I figured that might take time. I was grateful for small blessings. We had some make-up sex, and along came Caroline. About the time I had come home with Caroline, Myron left a letter laying on the counter. I read it. He never knew. The letter said that he had fulfilled the requirements to have expunged a charge of driving under the influence and with an open container." Ma looked away and took a breath. "Soon Myron was drinking harder then ever. He became more abusive. The neighbors never got involved. People figured that we were stand-offish. You've seen how they are. They assumed that we wanted our privacy, and they respected that. I taught the girls to say nothing to anyone about our family. I trained them not to provoke their father. The abuse just got worse. Soon, it became normal. I was scared to leave because I had no one else. I had nowhere else. Last night I reached my limit. If I die for it, my daughters will have a better life." Ma trembled and began crying. Vinnie's father moved to her side, drew her to his chest and held her. Mrs. Il-Cazzo pulled me to her side as Vinnie and Caroline returned.

"All clear on every side." Vinnie saluted his father.

He walked away, and the fire had returned to his eyes. I started to follow, but he held up a hand. Vinnie stood by a tree scanning the parking lot, and Otis walked over to him chucking him on the shoulder. They spoke for a moment, and he handed Vinnie a knife. Vinnie pushed a button and a blade snapped out. Vinnie played with the knife reversing the grip a few times.

Otis came back and hugged me and Caroline. He gave Ma a kiss on the cheek. "Take care. Stay safe." He walked away and climbed into a car.

Tori approached Vinnie and put an arm around his shoulder. She had a twenty ounce Sprite bottle in her purse. Vinnie took the bottle and had a good pull. He took two more, and his body relaxed. They walked back, Vinnie's eyes were different. They looked a bit glassy, but gentle. We climbed into the van, and he fell asleep with his arms around me, and Caroline's face in his lap as she napped.

I was breathing deeply -- half asleep -- and enjoying the spicy fragrance of Vinnie's cologne, when two hours later we pulled into a hotel. It was a two story horseshoe with plenty of parking. Most of the slots were occupied. The place was an off-chain establishment, plain looking and built of stuccoed blocks, painted a faded pink, with iron stairs and railings that were painted white. Vinnie's father informed us that several support networks used the place while moving abused spouses across the nation. Pat had given him the location.

Vinnie entered the lobby with his father and secured a second-story room with a view of the parking lot. The Il-Cazzos and Bakers moved in for the night, and Vinnie's father set up a chair by the window to watch for police. Tori chatted with her mother while Vinnie made sure that Caroline and I were comfortable. Ma lay down on one of the queen-sized beds, and Mrs. Il-Cazzo helped to prop her head on some pillows.

"So, dolls, me and Tori need to cut out and pull a scout detail. We're going to pound our ground smashers to a food emporium and load up on comestibles. You stick here and stay away from the windows." Vinnie handed Caroline the remote and winked at me. I blushed and nodded.

Forty-five minutes later Vinnie and Tori returned with two grocery bags loaded with enough junk food to give Slim Good-body a heart attack. Tori started the coffee, and Vinnie sat on a bed next to Caroline. I snuggled into his arms as we watched a cooking show on television. My sense of smell has always been keen, and Vinnie's clothes carried a faint odor of a skunk, or maybe sweat. I had never smelled the odor before, and it didn't mix well with the scent of his cologne. I didn't say anything at the time. He was mellow, and loose, which was better than the intensity he had exuded that entire day.

Ma insisted that she felt better, but Vinnie's mother told her to keep resting.

After icing Ma's head a bit, Mrs. Il-Cazzo suggested they sleep. Caroline and I were drinking milk, and eating Fritos and bean dip, while watching some chefs cook for judges. Vinnie fell asleep holding me between his legs with his arms wrapped around my chest.

He woke up two hours later, and we moved to a chair so that Tori could cuddle with Caroline and read her a bedtime story about David and Goliath from the Gideon Bible. After Caroline fell asleep, Tori positioned herself by the door and was asleep in minutes. Vinnie sat watch by the window with his father and drank coffee. I put two pillows under my butt on the floor beside him, resting against his legs, and dozed off.

Someone was in the room with us. Pa had found us and had his rifle. He was aiming at

Vinnie's face. Vinnie turned dark green, his shirt tearing as his body increased in size...

I sat bolt upright crying and screaming.

The room was as it had been. Everyone was safe. Lights flicked on. Vinnie moved down to sit by my side. He was still Vinnie.

"Shhh. It's OK. You're safe. No one's going to hurt you now. Vinnie's here." Vinnie stroked my cheek.

"I...I'm sorry. I should have fought back or behaved better or..." I whimpered.

Caroline climbed out of bed and walked over. Ma started getting up, but Vinnie's mother told her to lay still. Tori came over and sat with a wet washcloth on my face.

"It isn't your fault. You did nothing to be sorry for." Tori hugged me from behind. "You let it out, ok."

Vinnie put my head to his heart. "Last night, when Otis was conversing with you and Caroline, the way you defended yourselves and each other, that was out of sight. In the van when we first arrived at the shelter, you two had each other's back. I was impressed. You have sass, baby. You have the makings to survive this, straight from the fridge."

A half hour later Tori tucked Caroline back into bed and sat down beside her. Vinnie fell asleep sitting against a wall with my head on his lap.

There was a wooded area surrounding me, with a waterfall, and beautiful, fragrant flowers. Vinnie and I were alone, and naked. We stood hugging and kissing under the waterfall as birds sang to us. Vinnie reached down and...

I woke up six hours later with a smile on my face. Vinnie yawned and stroked my cheek. The others were shuffling around, taking out clothes, and packing up the snacks. I gave Vinnie a quick kiss, and took a clean outfit from a suitcase.

After everyone was showered, we checked out. Vinnie shoved the extra rolls of potty tissue into his backpack, and extracted a fat envelope. He pulled two gift cards for IHOP from a bundle. Before checking out we raided the donuts and juice.

Vinnie's father drove us to the state line before locating an IHOP. We parked in the rear of the lot, and I noticed that Vinnie's father had left the keys in the front seat. I looked at Vinnie, but he shrugged. He put an arm around Ma's waist and the other around my shoulders. Tori and Caroline followed, and then Vinnie's parents. We were greeted by a short, plump, African- American lady who led us to a table in the back. Vinnie sat next to me facing the entire restaurant with our backs against a wall. He kept one hand in my lap, stroking me, and the other on the table.

"Want some coffee, doll? Caroline?" Vinnie poured a mug for himself and Tori.

"I don't know if we're allowed. Pa never let us." My raspy voice was improving. I looked at Ma.

"You probably won't like the taste, but go right ahead. The rules have changed a bit." Ma gave us a wan smile.

Vinnie refilled Tori's cup and filled mugs for me and Caroline. I added cream and sugar before tasting it. The taste was strong, acrid, but enjoyable. Caroline made a yucky face and pushed hers away.

"I guess coffee isn't your cup of tea.

You'll develop a taste after a while. You seem to enjoy it though, babe." Vinnie looked at Caroline and then at me. "By the way, if someone is ever bothering you, I mean in a threatening way, and you happen to have coffee in your cup, dump it in his lap." Vinnie chuckled. "Or throw it in his eyes."

"Yeah, and then slam the mug across the side of his head. Or, if you have a paper cup instead of a mug, take your hands and clap them hard on his ears," Tori nodded.

"What are you teaching them?" Ma glared.

"Some basic self defense. They could well use it. You too ma'am." Vinnie shrugged.

"Vincenzo! Torrence! Show a little respect for Mrs. Baker," their mother scolded. "I should think you might ask before telling her daughters such things. That might not be her way."

They lowered their eyes. "Sorry mama. Sorry Mrs. Baker." Everyone ate in silence until their father cleared his throat.

"Actually, honey, I might be to blame. I asked them to teach the girls some basics. Heather and they have a long road ahead. If anything happens it's for the best that they can survive on their own until help arrives." Vinnie's father looked at Ma. "But, my dear Antoinette is correct about respect. You're their mother and have full say so."

"I suppose it's fine. We need help, but I don't want my daughters becoming thugs. Young ladies, if you're in danger, then fighting is acceptable. Necessary even. So help me, if you even think about hurting other people without a reason, I will peel your butts. Don't even think about starting down that path. Fighting is a last resort." Ma groaned and held her head.

Caroline nodded and ate her food. I set

my coffee down. "Maybe if you had known how to fight we wouldn't be in this mess." I immediately regretted my words as Ma started crying.

"I'm sorry. I should have done more. You girls deserve better." Ma put her face in her hands. I looked down, and started crying, too.

"I dig that you felt stuck in the situational morass, but that's over. Isn't it better that I teach Steph and Caroline how to prevent a reoccurrence of the situation? I could teach you too, if you like." Vinnie put one arm around me, and one under the table in my lap. The pleasant feeling of him stroking my thigh helped my tears to diminish.

"I appreciate that, young man. I grew up believing that girls only fight if there is no other option. Stephanie's words sting, but she is correct. So yes, teach them what you can."

After everyone was finished Vinnie paid with the gift cards and instructed that the remaining balance be issued as a tip as well as leaving a twenty dollar bill under his coffee mug. Ma gave him a wary eye.

"Yes ma'am?" Vinnie gave her innocent.

"I noticed earlier that you have a great number of cards and coupons and such. You were sorting them at the hotel. Seems odd for a child is all."

Vinnie looked at his mother who nodded at him. "It's something I do to help out. It saves us money and you might try it when you get where you're heading. Survival is more than just kicking ass and taking names. I send emails to restaurants and manufacturers. I tell them my complaints. They send me vouchers, gift cards, and coupons. It works out well."

We walked out to the parking lot and the van was gone. Vinnie looked at his father who winked in return. When we got to the parking spot, all of our luggage had been placed inside of a 1969 model Plymouth Satellite station wagon. It looked old but clean.

"Friend of mine swapped with us."

Vinnie's father reassured us. "Should hold nine people comfortably, plus a family dog, and luggage."

"Guess that takes care of anyone tracking us." Tori giggled

"Old trick, kiddo." Mrs. Il-Cazzo chuckled.

We climbed in and got positioned. The adults sat up front, Tori and Caroline sat in the back seat, and Vinnie and I stretched out in the rear with the luggage. We lay there as Vinnie stroked my bruised butt and thighs under the cotton skirt I wore. His hand over my Hanes felt delicious and comforting. No one could see us unless they turned around. Mr Il-Cazzo tuned in an easy listening station and we drove away listening to Rex Smith sing "You Take My Breath Away." To all the world we appeared a family on vacation.

"What kind of tunes turn your crank?" Vinnie asked as I buried my face in his Neck, inhaling his scent. I sighed with contentment and held him closer.

"Taylor Swift, Zach Brown, Sugarland and Kenny Chesney. I don't get to listen to music too much. I like Jimmy Buffett too."

"Yeah, I dig Buffett. Country is cool. I can do without rap. Oldies like Billy Joel and Elton John are always a solid option. And I dig easy listening stuff like Mannilow or Zamfir. When I need to chill or want something in the background while I read, Zamfir is aces." Vinnie sat up with me and we rested our heads on the back seat.

"Who's Zamfir? And what is that cologne you wear? I love the smell of it."

"It's Aramis. I get a shipment every month from some cats my father knows. As for Zamfir, they call him master of the pan pipes. He's an acquired taste, but I dig his stuff." Vinnie grabbed his sack and removed an iPod. "Here, tune your ears in."

I sat listening on earbuds and smiling.

The music was haunting, in a soothing sort of way. In a few minutes my eyes closed and I fell asleep with my face in Vinnie's lap. Five hours later we pulled off the highway and down a smaller road. I was laying next to Vinnie, stroking his chest as he stroked mine. We sat up as the station wagon slowed.

"All right folks, we disembark here, spend the night and tomorrow visit my eldest daughter. After that it's a straight shot to The Magic Kingdom." Vinnie's father climbed out.

We eased out, and Vinnie had a good stretch before reaching for his sack. We followed the others into the lobby of a motel.

Mrs. Il-Cazzo leaned over to Ma. "Watch and learn. You never pay full price at a motel like this, and you'll be staying at many of these low level places. It's a lot safer and far more anonymous. Plus, it's much cheaper." They approached the front desk.

Vinnie's mother pushed a bell on the counter, and a lady in a severe looking black skirt suit came out of an office. She had olive skin, a tight bun in her jet black hair, and no visible makeup.

"Could I get a room for the night?"

"We have rooms available. You'll be wanting two of them? Adjoining? One hundred and twenty dollars for both."

"We need one room, and thirty dollars for the night. I doubt you get much business here, and I'm paying cash." Vinnie's mother stared at the clerk."

"Too many for one room. I can do one hundred for both."

"I suppose we can go down the road. You aren't the only game in town." Mrs. Il-Cazzo turned toward us as if to leave.

"I really shouldn't do this, but I see your point. OK. Fifty dollars." The lady was annoyed, but then semi-smiled when Vinnie's mother handed her the cash. "Room 203. If you need anything, call the front desk. It is only me and my husband working here and he handles the maintenance. You need anything, you call and ask for Phil Lazio." She pointed to a name plate on a door behind her."

"What's that?" Vinnie's father was standing back with the rest of us,

"Not suitable for children's ears." Mrs. Il-Cazzo muttered and took our key.

Vinnie was trying not to laugh, so Tori elbowed him in the ribs. I didn't understand what was so funny.

We left the office and took the stairs. The room was sparse, but it had everything we needed. There were two queen beds covered in white sheets and crimson comforters. The pillows on the beds were fluffy. A television was affixed to the dresser to discourage removal. There was a desk with an office chair.

"OK, everyone." Vinnie's father smiled.

"The plan is to leave our luggage here. I Spotted a Walmart on the way over. If you ladies need anything, extra shorts, shirts, anything, I'm buying. Also since we'll be traveling without many stops tomorrow, we might want some comestibles to pack out. Crackers, candy, stuff like that."

"You don't have to buy us clothes." Ma looked uncomfortable.

"No, I don't. I want to, though. About time someone took care of you."

"If you insist, I won't refuse. You did a real number on the lady downstairs. I doubt I could be so pushy."

"Sure you can. It just takes practice." Tori laughed. "As Mama and Papa always say, never argue with a woman if you can dicker instead."

We left the room and walked three blocks to a Super-Walmart. Vinnie and I took point. We held hands, and Vinnie held a closed knife in his left hand. Tori was behind us with Caroline, and the adults brought up the rear. Nothing happened, but Vinnie scanned the area with every step.

After selecting a cart, Ma, Caroline, and I took the lead. Vinnie's parents and Tori brought up the rear. Vinnie was looking at posters of missing children. He caught up with us as Ma was picking out underwear and socks.

"Hey, if burgers sound good for lunch, I have vouchers for free meals. I also have a whole mess of coupons for food." Vinnie smiled as Ma gave him a concerned look.

"That sounds fine." Ma moved to a rack of shirts and shorts.

Vinnie turned toward me and Caroline.

"Hey, while your mama picks out clothes, You and Caroline want a couple board games or something? Helps to pass the boring hours."

I gave Vinnie a hug. Caroline's eyes widened as her mouth turned up. Ma started to object, but then gave in. Tori and Vinnie walked with me and Caroline to the toy aisle. We chose Sorry and Scrabble. In the book aisle Vinnie purchased a copy of the first Twilight book for me and bought Caroline a Harry Potter book. He rolled his eyes, but put them in the cart.

"You don't like these books?" I looked at Vinnie with my head tilted to the side.

"Not my taste, but opinions vary. Now this is a book that'll knock your socks off." He picked up a copy of *In Broad Daylight* by Harry

N. MacLean. "This is a solid read. Real time stuff, and totally hard-core."

"I'll read it. So you don't like vampires and wizards?"

"I do, but Bram Stoker did it first and best. If you want wizards, try *Le Mort d'Arthur*."

Tori hook her head, laughing. "Don't mind him. He has sophisticated literary tastes, and he's set in his ways."

Vinnie stuck out his tongue at her as she giggled.

We found Ma talking with Vinnie's parents. We pushed the well loaded cart to the luggage aisle where Ma picked out a giant purple rolling suitcase. After that we wandered through the grocery section and Vinnie pulled out his envelope of coupons.

"Tell me again, Vinnie. Where did you get all of those?" Ma's mouth turned down at the corners as her eyes narrowed. The look Caroline and I got when we misbehaved.

"I can show you rather than tell you. I've had my finger on the action for years now. Hey, Steph, grab a bag of chips. Whatever flavor you like. Caroline, grab a pack of cookies."

Tori gave me a big smile, and Mrs. Il-Cazzo nodded. Ma looked confused. I brought over a bag of corn chips and a Caroline grabbed a package of fudge stripe cookies. Vinnie took them and handed the chips to Caroline. He put the cookies in the cart.

"Read the back of that bag, please. There should be something on the bottom with a phone number." Vinnie smiled at Caroline and winked at Ma.

Caroline studied the bag. "Oh yeah, here. *If you are not completely satisfied withthis product, feel free to call our corporate office or email for a replacement.*" She put the bag in the cart.

"All products have a variation on that. If you've got an address they send you coupons that make purchases free or almost free." Vinnie chuckled. "If you have several addresses you get more. A post office box, and several friends works well. You have the friends forward your mail. Except for a while your friends oughtn't know where you are."

Ma's eyes narrowed again, and her cheeks turned red. "Does the word scoundrel mean anything to you, young man?"

Vinnie shrugged. His parents roared in delight, and Tori looked at Ma. "You ain't heard nothing yet, ma'am." Tori giggled. "Baby brother here is a genius at this."

We bought eight bags full of snack foods and drinks. Vinnie paid, and with coupons the cost of the groceries was $8.32. The clothes, toiletries and other items brought the total to $193.76. Mr. Il-Cazzo used a Visa gift card to pay the balance.

"There are other ways to get clothes for free, but one step at a time." Vinnie's father pushed the cart.

We walked to a fast food restaurant near the Walmart exit. After what had just occurred, I was looking at Vinnie differently. He had looks, but he also had brains. It was clear that he read a lot, and well beyond our grade level, but he also had a certain ingenuity that turned me on. I knew that Ma didn't approve of his behavior, and maybe that was part of the excitement.

As Ma, and Vinnie's parents packed the new suitcase at a table, Tori, Vinnie, Caroline, and I ordered value meals, extra chicken nuggets, and desserts. Using vouchers we paid nothing. It was a large quantity of food, and yet the counter person didn't even blink at the stack of vouchers,

After returning to the table, we dug in. I stared at Vinnie, and grinned. "You didn't even have to pay! How do you get restaurant coupons?"

Vinnie shrugged. "That takes a bit more creativity, doll. Keep the peepers peeled for corporate feedbags that get big turnover. Not exclusively in your city, but all over the nation. I get on the squawk-box and tell them I got an order to go. I asked for no onions but they put the onions on my sandwich. Usually the manager sends a few vouchers for free sandwiches or free meals. All the major chains do it. Even steakhouses and seafood restaurants send vouchers to replace messed up orders."

"Well, if they make a mistake then they should fix it." Caroline chimed in.

Vinnie chuckled. "Straight from the fridge, kid. Except that most of the time you're telling them they did, even if they didn't. These places are corporations. They charge a lot of money, and don't pay their employees anything like enough. So a few free vouchers helps us and doesn't hurt them." He drank soda. "It's the urban pirate way. It'd be a crime not to plunder them."

"You mean that you lie and justify it to yourself?" Ma gave Vinnie the look me and Caroline got just before she sent us to our room for a time-out.

Mr. Il-Cazzo rolled his eyes and shook his head. Mrs. Il-Cazzo and Tori grinned.

"Call it what you will. I'm Robin Hood. I'm also the poor. Anyhow, it gets trickier." Vinnie cleared his throat. "One can also call directly to a restaurant and often the manager asks you to come in for a meal on the house. In those cases it's always the rule to duke the server at least fifty percent of the cost of the meal, and, if possible, closer to seventy-five percent. That way the server is getting the bread instead of the corporate office." Vinnie began eating his sundae as I belched and giggled.

"Excuse yourself, young lady!" Ma admonished.

"Excuse me. I think I ate too fast." I giggled more. Vinnie gave me the feels.

"So you people are low level scam artists, but you have a slight moral code." Ma shook her head at the Il-Cazzos. "Well, you couldn't have picked a better town to live in. No one ever reports anything, even if they should. I suppose if your scam works and you need food..."

"That's my thinking," Vinnie interrupted.

"and I don't identify as a scam artist. I'm A pirate, but I operate on dry land for now."

Vinnie's parents nodded and Tori put an arm around his shoulders. "Pirates forever and always!" Tori raised a fist in the air.

We finished, and cleared the table.

Vinnie insisted that we top off our cups Before returning to the motel and settling in. He pointed out that the soda was free. Ma lay down for a nap with Caroline. I started reading *In*

Broad Daylight. Vinnie was right, it was a great book and an exciting story.

Vinnie was staring into space, troubled. He excused himself to go for a quick walk. Mr. Il-Cazzo told him to be cautious and to check the neighborhood for any heavy police presence. Vinnie left, and Tori followed him. I considered asking Ma if we could move to Skidmore, Missouri. Those people knew how to stop monsters like Pa.

An hour later, Vinnie and Tori knocked a signal. Vinnie had the glassy look in his eyes again, and sat against a wall napping. His father and mother were on a bed sleeping. Tori sat looking out a window. I moved over and snuggled into Vinnie as I read. He had the skunk smell on his clothes again, too.

A strange sensation crept into my brain over the next few hours. Instead of being on pins and needles, afraid of being found, I was viewing our escape as a fun trip. It was as if our families had decided to go away for a few days. Pa wasn't around, and thinking about him returned me to the moment, but otherwise my mind had relaxed.

Vinnie woke up at five, and the others a half hour later. Everyone piled into the station wagon and we headed east to a diner. It was an honest to goodness, comfort food, jukebox in the corner, sort of place.

I was perusing the menu when Caroline asked if she could play the jukebox. There were a few other couples in the place and some music was already playing. Vinnie took out his wallet and handed Caroline and me each five dollars to play some songs. Ma walked over with us and even picked out a few songs. We giggled as she grew excited over a band called Stray Cats and one called The Ramones.

Tori and Vinnie ordered huge chicken meals, and a pot of coffee. I had never met anyone who ate as much as Vinnie, at least not without gaining a lot of weight. His parents had salad, pork chops, and club soda. Ma, Caroline, and I ordered cheeseburgers and french fries with Cokes.

As everyone was digesting after the meal, Kenny Rogers "She Believes in Me" Started playing. Vinnie stood and took me by the hand. We stepped away from the table and danced. Dancing together, my arms wrapped around Vinnie, aroused feelings in me that I couldn't explain. Everything about him did, and the feelings were stronger the more time we spent together.

"All My Exes Live in Texas" played next and we danced to that as well. Vinnie dipped me as a series of faster paced rock and roll songs brought our entire group to their feet. Vinnie's father was dancing with Ma, his mother with Caroline and Tori. Vinnie swung me around his body and slid me between his legs as "Rock This Town" by The Stray Cats filled the air. Vinnie turned toward Caroline, lifting her off her feet, swinging her this way and that to her delighted giggling. He finished the evening by doing the jitterbug with Tori. I swear, he had it all.

At nine we returned to our room and fell asleep. Vinnie's father sat watch by the window, while Vinnie slept on the floor with my face in his lap. This almost seemed like normal fun. If nightmares hadn't woken me every hour or so, I would have been having a blast.

The next morning, after grabbing donuts, coffee, and juice in the lobby, we packed the station wagon and drove across town. Tori and Vinnie were in the backseat with me and Caroline. I leaned against Vinnie, falling in love, hoping that he could stay with me forever. A lot of people say that one can't fall in love at the age of twelve. Well, I did.

"Steph? I wanted to give you something. You too, Caroline." Vinnie smiled at us.

Tori looked at him as he whipped something hard out of his pants.

"If you get separated from your mama, doll, keep this club handy. If anyone tries anything funny, you use it. Don't club with it, though. Taking a back swing is less effective. Leave it collapsed as it is now and jam it as hard as you can into the crotch or the solar plexus. Then, after that, pop this side button and snap it open. I'll demonstrate later. Once open, swing it like you were delivering a slap to the face. Straight across the left side of the head or body. Yes, it may well bring about death. Better him than you."

I shuddered and nodded. Caroline shrunk down her eyes wide, her lips trembling. For all our tough talk at the shelter, we were both scared to death. We'd been trained in fear, steeped in terror.

Vinnie slipped me the baton, and looked at Caroline. "I think you'd be better with a whistle, and an airhorn. If you have problems, pull the strip from the airhorn and press the button aiming it at the creeps ears. After that blow this police whistle and run at the same time. Get inside the nearest store and scream that you're being hurt. You'll involve the police, but that may be unavoidable." Caroline nodded at Vinnie. "I can buy you an airhorn later at a store," he ruffled Caroline's hair and handed her a metal whistle.

Ma looked back at us. "I appreciate the need for this, I suppose. You're acting like we're heading to war, though."

"You are." Vinnie and his father said simultaneously. Mrs. Il-Cazzo chuckled.

"You're engaged in custodial kidnapping. There's a possibility that an Amber Alert might be out, although for several reasons I doubt it. The likelihood of police looking for you is high back home. Therefore, returning there isn't advisable. The only option is to move forward, alone, and without standard resources. Knowing how to eat cheap or free, clothe and supply yourself, and how to defend yourself is not without reason. You are, in fact, at war. Trust no one to be on your side." Vinnie's father pulled into a parking lot and made a call on his cell phone.

Ten minutes later Vinnie's sister Gina appeared from behind a building. I'd only seen her a few times before she moved away from their house. She was dressed in a long, loose, patchwork skirt and a light blue t-shirt over which she wore a denim vest. Her blonde hair was long and matted. It resembled clumped straw Tori and Vinnie ran over. "Gina! Hey, we've missed you!" They hugged her and she returned the hugs with interest.

"Well, look what blows in when we leave the doors open." Gina giggled at Tori.

Their parents approached, hugging and kissing Gina who was all smiles.

"Great to see you guys! What's shaking?

You were pretty cryptic on the phone, papa. And, who's this?" Gina motioned at Ma, Caroline, and me.

We walked along a path by brick and stone buildings. Vinnie's mother filled in Gina as we approached the campus commons. We ventured inside a building, and Gina led everyone into a study room before locking the door. "It's soundproofed," she said.

Gina asked a series of questions and Ma answered them. After that was done, Gina filled everyone in on college life.

"Life around here is aces" Gina told us.

"On my first day I found two computer labs and a small library that remain open day and night. There are study rooms attached. I keep a blanket and pillow at a friend's dorm room and retrieve them at night. I study until midnight or one in the morning and then crash on the floor of a study room. I can sleep until seven. After that I return the bedding to my friend. The gym has showers and the cafeterias have an all you can eat policy. I purchased the minimum food point plan and carry out fruit, cereal and sandwiches in my backpack. I use empty soda bottles to carry out juice as well. I even audit courses for free so that I can try to test out of them later." Gina blushed when when her father ruffled her hair.

"You OK for clothes?" Mrs. Il-Cazzo looked concerned.

"Natch. You raised me didn't you?

There's a Salvation Army store in town, and also an old, reconverted warehouse where people drop off clothing to be given away free to the needy. They permit people to sign in and take two outfits a week. Plus, through donations, they have entire packages of new underclothes and socks to give away." Gina laughed.

I made a mental note to ask Vinnie about the clothing places, and about using colleges to hide for the night. I wondered if I could sneak into the cafeterias without ID. I looked up at Ma, and reconsidered my options.

Vinnie was hanging on Gina's every word.

I swear he was taking mental notes, himself, on how to game the system. Something in that excited me. Vinnie acted as if the world was a game to beat. As if life was a sheep to be fleeced. I wanted to join him in that. We could be Bonnie and Clyde.

A half hour later we walked as a group toward a men's dorm. Mr. Il-Cazzo explained something to Gina in hushed tones, and slipped her a small fold of bills. She walked inside as we stood around. When she came out an hour later she handed her father three plastic cards.

Mr. Il-Cazzo turned toward Ma, and handed her the cards. "After we reach our final destination, you'll need new ID cards. Yours is a Wisconsin drivers license. You are Marion Arnaque. Your eldest is Laverne and her sister is Shirley. Nod and agree that you watch too many TV reruns if anyone asks."

"Where did you get these pictures of us?" Ma looked at the cards.

"I took them with my cell phone. It stays on silent so you never even knew." Vinnie's mother shrugged. " That does present a potential danger. However, if someone texted your photo, as I did to Gina, you'd be gone before anyone could act on the information."

We left and went to a local Chinese buffet. While everyone was eating, Gina kept giving Vinnie strange looks. "What's the scam, Sam? Something on your mind?" Vinnie scowled.

"Let's go outside for a few minutes. I need some air" Gina excused herself and led Vinnie outside.

Outside the window I watched Gina standing with her arms crossed, irritation written on her face. Vinnie was gesticulating, aggravation written on his. They returned ten minutes later, and Vinnie grabbed his sack. He walked to the dessert buffet, and filled up several ziplock bags.

That afternoon we said our farewells, and Vinnie's mother took a bunch of photos of everyone. We piled into the station wagon, and Mr. Il-Cazzo drove south. As evening hit we stopped for dinner at a pizza parlor paid for with Vinnie's vouchers. Afterward, Tori and Caroline laid down in the backseat to sleep. Vinnie slept with me amongst the luggage, our hands between each other's legs. The adults sat up front with Vinnie's father driving, and Ma and Mrs Il-Cazzo sleeping sitting up.

"What was that with your sister earlier?" I whispered.

"Nothing. She worries too much about

things. So does Tori. I can handle things. I have been since I was eight. It's cool." He whispered back.

"Since you were eight? Where were your ma and pa?"

"They had some issues going on with dark thoughts, and too much mental pressure. It got handled. That was before we moved down the block from you. Things are cool now. Copacetic."

"I'm glad we're together. Can you teach me how to get vouchers and stuff?"

"Sure, doll. I'll teach you everything."

"Is using colleges to hideout safe?"

"Let me noodle that out? My gut instinct is no, because security would ask questions about you and Caroline. There might be a way, but I'd need to chew on it."

"Is Salvation Army good for clothes?"

"Posilutely. That, Ill teach you when we have time."

We kissed, and snuggled closer. Seven hours later Vinnie moved away from me. I figured he was going potty, but he was gone for a while. I sat up and climbed out of the station wagon. Caroline was still asleep, as were the adults. Vinnie was in the middle of a strenuous workout with Tori. He was bare chested and stripped down to loose denim shorts. Tori was in a running top and jogging shorts. They were engaged in a martial arts fight.

I stood watching, and Caroline climbed out to stand beside me. Vinnie and Tori demonstrated some moves for us, and had us imitate them. Vinnie showed me how to release the collapsible steel baton. He also demonstrated how to deliver a strike to the knees with it, and some head strikes.

"Doll, if you take the strongest and tallest man on earth and crush his knees, he'll fall. Then it's a lot easier to seal his fate, or run away." Vinnie slipped me the baton.

"I don't know if I could. What if I freeze up?"

"You won't. There's something inside of you. I've seen it. If you have to fight, you'll win. You are done being pushed around. Repeat that to yourself until you believe it."

After the self defense lessons we found some dirty, but serviceable, shower stalls and rinsed off. The water required a quarter for five minutes. I thought about joining Vinnie in a shower stall, but I was sure that I wouldn't enjoy the response from Ma if we got caught.

After a breakfast of eggs, bacon, and cheese grits at a diner, we crossed into another state.

We stopped at a used book store a half

hour later, right as the proprietor was hanging an open sign. Vinnie asked if we could look inside. The place smelled like dry oatmeal, and Vinnie looked like he was in Heaven. He perused the true crime section, and I wandered to the history section. Vinnie and his father joined me.

Vinnie purchased several books, and I picked out *Trials of The Earth* by Mary Hamilton. Caroline opted for *Pippi Longstocking* by Astrid Lindgrin. Ma chose some romance novels. Vinnie paid for their books, and handed me a copy of *Catch Me If You Can* by Frank Abagnale.

"This is a great read, doll. Abagnale sold out on the cause, but understanding the way he operated will hip you to my lick and to where my wig is at."

I giggled. "Thank you, Vinnie." I hugged him and snuck in a quick kiss.

Three hours later we were in the town of Spectacle, more a series of themed resorts than an actual town. Vinnie's father had been on his phone texting most of that time. We arrived at a resort that was built to look like something out of *Gone With The Wind*. The place was exquisite, and the room we were in had pictures that lit up like stars in the sky when a button was pushed. There were pictures everywhere of ladies dressed in gowns and hoop skirts. In a kitschy way, the room was beautiful. Caroline was in her element, and we had fun playing with the lights on the pictures.

Vinnie, Caroline, and I went exploring outside with Tori while the adults rested. We discovered giant hammocks near one of the pools. Caroline and Tori climbed into one, while Vinnie and I lay in the other.

Vinnie whistled low, his eyes lighting up.

"This is too cool for school, gate. This whole place is perfectly arranged so that paying to stay, or not, a cat could catch a nap, hit the pool, and be entertained for free."

"They'd need to have lanyard cards that were registered, wouldn't they?" Caroline looked over. Tori smiled and shook her head.

"This entire place is wide open with regards to security, doll," Vinnie chuckled with Tori. "True, we have cards that show we're paying guests, but, did you notice that the same cards are for sale in the gift shop in other colors and designs?"

"Yeah? So?" I snuggled into Vinnie.

"So, a card and lanyard can be pocketed with ease. That means that any stranger willing to play it in a minor chord, and dress in a presentable fashion, can use any of the Spectacle resort pools, and find places to nap free of charge. This is an urban pirate's wet dream."

"You mean stealing from the store?"

Caroline was shocked. "I wouldn't sit for a month if Ma caught me shoplifting."

"It isn't shoplifting, doll. The corporations call it shrink. It's like I'm helping them to lose weight. I help grocery stores reduce a whole lot more. Anyway, in this case, one could return the card after they were done. You'd only need it to ward off nosy staff."

I giggled. "You're something else, Vinnie. You make me laugh, and forget my troubles."

Vinnie gave me a cuddle and sighed. "I wish we had more time together. I'm feeling it now. It took disaster, but it took what it took to get close to you."

Tori and Caroline stood. "Let's go walk around." Tori held Caroline's hand.

At one spot on the north side there was an entry through a wooded glen. This was not a resort design, but rather an open space off of a main road. We cut through, and after walking along the roads and stretching our legs, we discovered a major highway and several apartment complexes behind some fences.

"I'd bet plenty that employees jungle up in those complexes, and hoof it to work which would explain the unguarded opening to the resort." Vinnie rubbed his chin with a thumb.

"You have everything figured out. You're really smart, Vinnie." I was amazed.

"He's our parents' son. Especially Papa's. We've been raised to notice things like this." Tori smiled.

"Ma thinks you're scoundrels." Caroline giggled.

"Nuts to her. We have more going on than the average Clyde, and we can survive anything that comes our way. You two should learn how to observe, and how to use what you observe." Tori shook her head.

I pointed at a spot on the fence. "There's a big hole over there. If I was careful and crawled through I could get into those apartments."

"Why for?" Vinnie nodded at me.

"There's some benches, if I needed a place to rest. If I lived there and wanted to sneak away after Ma went to bed, too. You know, to make time with my boyfriend." I blushed.

"Make time?" Tori giggled.

"I read it in a book, once. I think it means something romantic."

Tori nodded. "It does. Ummm...Steph, has your mama had the talk with you guys?"

I looked at Caroline and shrugged. 'No, but I learned things in class at school. I explained it to sissy. She was grossed out, but I'm interested."

Caroline stuck out her tongue. "Yuck! I can't believe people do that."

Vinnie rubbed her head. "Believe it. If they didn't, there'd be no Caroline or Steph."

I looked away. "Maybe that'd be better. Maybe then Pa wouldn't..."

Tori turned me toward her. "No. No, Steph. You are *not* to blame for his actions. Neither of you are. He's a creep from creepsville, and he'll pay for it. You are not to blame."

Vinnie hugged me close as we walked back to our resort. As we crossed an area by the main lobby, I spotted a sign.

"Hey, this resort has free movies and entertainment each night. So do the other resorts. The trolley's to other resorts are free, too. If you lived in those apartments, or anywhere, you could walk here and see free stuff every night."

Vinnie hugged me so tight I thought my ribs might give out. "Hot damn, she might be a pirate yet. Yes, exactly. You could drive from anywhere, park in those apartments, and utilize the entertainment resources like gangbusters."

As we walked, I noticed Vinnie's expression changing. He kept looking back toward where we had exited and entered. That evening in the pool with his father, I discovered why he looked concerned. The others were swimming, while Vinnie, his father, and I lounged in the shallow area.

"Papa, you and mama have always taught me to look a place over and to decide if the area is safe. This resort isn't and the other accessible resorts aren't." Vinnie opened the conversation as his father's eyebrows raised.

I looked at them, concerned. "We aren't safe here?"

"We are, doll, but the area around, here not so much,"

"In what way, son?" His father nodded at him to continue.

"Well, earlier Steph, Caroline, Tori, and I were walking. We saw several places were one could access this resort from an open road. It's a busy road, but no one seems to even stop and look at strangers appearing out of the woods. I would think that someone with evil intent could walk in as well."

"Evil intent? You mean like pirates?" I giggled.

"Hey, now. Pirates are the good guys in my book. Anyway, no. I mean terrorists." Vinnie gave me a serious stare.

"Interesting. Walk me through it, son." Vinnie's father nodded.

"Well, I've read about these things from the eighties called SADMs. Man portable nuclear devices that fit in a backpack and weigh sixty pounds at most. One can find the process to build them on the Internet. So, let's say I'm a super rich foreigner and I build ten. I have ten men walk onto the grounds separately, and ride the busses to various resorts or restaurants in Spectacle. At a specified time they set those off. Imagine that. Or, even less dramatic than nuclear, a regular bomb with enough power to blow apart a room."

I gasped. Mr. Il-Cazzo looked thoughtful.

"I see your point, son. Of course the Same situation holds true for any of the super-cinemas that exist in America or for almost anywhere, except airports, bus terminals or train stations. I agree, however, that as a tourist draw for people from all over the world, Spectacle is a prime target for starting a world war." His father smiled at us. "You have an exceptionally focused mind, son."

"That's kind of paranoid isn't it?" I was worried.

"I'm kind of paranoid most of the time," Vinnie gave me a wink, "but hey, let's go swim and forget about it."

We started swimming toward Caroline and Tori. The afternoon was a blast. We joined in the poolside activities set up by the staff members, swam, and forgot our troubles.

After swimming, Vinnie's parents led our group to the cafeteria. The people who ran the area had a system in place intended to charge each guest for a refillable soda mug good for their entire stay. The price was quite steep, especially to people like the Il-Cazzos who were in the habit of paying rarely, if ever, for anything. Vinnie's father purchased one mug. He then took six more mugs from the cafeteria over the course of a half hour. By filling his mug he could refill the others. The machines limited mug refills to one and a half mugs before insisting on a three minute wait, but his plan was possible. The machines also had a sensor that indicated if a mug had been registered at purchase. And, wouldn't you know, one of the soda machines wasn't registering whether the mug had been set with a resort code, and wasn't limiting refills. We filled our mugs to our hearts content. Ma looked irritated, and then, with an exasperated laugh, joined in. Spectacle was the sort of place a guy like Vinnie could thrive. I pointed out that the coffee and six different varieties of iced tea were free and had no mechanism to check mug registration.

"Great observation, gorgeous." Vinnie hugged me.

"Stephanie Ann!" Ma scolded. "I know it's there way, but so help me if you start getting dishonest. I raised you better, young lady. No offense to you, Frank and Antoinette, but that isn't how I want my daughters behaving."

"To each his own, Heather," Mrs. Il-Cazzo shrugged. "No offense taken." I sat and sulked for a bit, but refilled my soda twice as much after being chastised. I figured that Vinnie knew how to survive, and that we were going to need those skills. Ma didn't understand. I wasn't about to argue, though. I didn't know what she might do -- in public or not.

That evening we took a bus to a swank resort called The Spectacular where the concierge said we could watch free of charge as fireworks exploded across a lake. The men who greeted us as we departed the bus were dressed in top hats, old fashioned tuxedos, spats and white gloves. The inside of the resort was gorgeous, with crystal chandeliers and elegant, gilt architecture. The ambiance and decor were from the time period of the early twentieth century, around the time of the Titanic. I had seen the movie on TV, and the feel was right for that. There was a jazz quintet playing in the middle of the lobby surrounded by settees, couches and well crafted chairs. I decided that

Vinnie and I should run away and spend forever in a place such as that.

Vinnie's eyes were like saucers as he looked around. "This is what I aspire to. This right here. This kind of elegance is worthy of my pirating talents."

We made our way through the lobby, and paused for a moment when Vinnie took my hand and waltzed with me to the music from the quintet. After drawing applause from our families, and some onlookers, we found a spot outdoors and sat on benches and chairs. The fireworks were indeed spectacular and we all oohed and wowed. While we watched, I felt Vinnie's hand inch down my loose running shorts and rub my bottom. No one noticed, and I hid my pleasure in the midst of the gasps of the crowd.

Afterward, while looking for a bathroom, Vinnie entered an elevator and disappeared. He re-emerged ten minutes later from a doorway that hid a staircase with a cup of coffee in his hands, and a small plate of pastries. Vinnie handed Tori his cup of coffee and winked at her. She sipped and her eyes widened. I took an offered mini-éclair as did Caroline.

"I don't know where I just was, papa," Vinnie looked at his father. "I was looking for the restroom sign, and this lady put a card into a slot in the elevator. When we arrived, there was a huge smorgasbord set up. Meats, cheeses, crudités, and like fifteen kinds of coffee. I helped myself from the dessert selections." He popped a chocolate covered strawberry in his mouth.

"Remember how you did that, son. You just happened upon free access to the VIP level. People pay plenty extra for that level, and honestly, except for the free nosh and being checked in a bit faster, the rooms aren't that much nicer. Even so, free nosh that is genuinely free is not something one should pass up."

Tori giggled, loose and silly. "The coffee sure is grand. Strong too." She winked at Vinnie.

"Yeah, it said it was from Ireland, I think. Irish coffee."

We caught the bus back to our suite and fell asleep. Vinnie's father slept between Ma, and Mrs. Il-Cazzo. Caroline shared a bed with Tori while Vinnie and I shared a fold out couch. For the first time in days, I didn't dream about Pa hurting me. My dreams were filled with people dancing in grand ballrooms, Vinnie and I dancing in front of the fireworks, and Vinnie and I holding each other as people waited on us with trays of coffee and food.

The next morning I woke up with a hollow feeling in the pit of my stomach. This was the day that Ma, Caroline, and I were meeting some people who would drive us west and the north a bit. Ma had explained it to me. We were going to see my grandparents, and then decide where to go. I wouldn't see Vinnie for a long while, maybe never again.

Once everyone was awake, Vinnie asked if he and I could go for a walk together before breakfast. The adults said it was OK. Tori gave us a wary look, but said nothing. Vinnie and I walked out the door and around the property.

"I feel weird saying this, doll, but I love you. I mean forever love you. Head over heels, top of the ninth with bases loaded, love you." Vinnie nudged me inside of a single unit family bathroom and locked the door.

"I love you too, Vinnie. You saved my life. I'll always love you. Umm...I don't need the potty."

It's not the romantic place I would have preferred, doll, but it's as private as we can get. In a matter of moments I was in his arms, warm, soft, and fragile. My lips parted as did his and our tongues explored each other. We stood there for a few minutes kissing and hugging. His hands rubbed my jeans in the rear, and I moaned.

"Vinnie, we can't. Not here. Not now. I want to, but I want to somewhere nice. Like in the movies. Can't you and I run away?"

"Would that we could, but no. Stephanie Ann Baker, I will never forget you. One day I promise, I'm going to find you again. I wish we had more time right now. I'm going to find you, and light you up like a pinball machine. I swear it, baby." He gazed into my eyes as tears dripped down my face.

"Vincenzo Cassiel Michelangelo Il-Cazzo, you saved me. I would do anything for you. But Ma, Caroline, and I have to keep moving. You said so. Your family said so. I hope you do come find me in a few years. I won't let another boy near me until you do." I hugged Vinnie and cried. He comforted me.

We walked back to the suite, had showers, and changed our clothes before walking to the cafeteria area for breakfast. While we were devouring our platters of bacon, and waffles the size of a plate, Vinnie's father removed a small stack of papers from a purse.

"Heather, I need you to read these and sign them. They're legal documents allowing a realty company I know of to clean, repair and sell your house. Don't worry about Myron, he won't interfere."

"But, how? How do you know that? And, how will I get my share of the money?" Ma looked wan and drawn out.

"The less you know the better. Please, trust me that things are handled. You can't return, though. These papers will be faxed to Hawaii, then to Nova Scotia and finally to a lawyer in Nantucket. Your property and money will be delivered to a safe drop. You'll be informed of the location at another time. There's a process for that as well."

After Ma signed the papers, and breakfast was devoured, we went to use the restrooms. Ma, Caroline, and I walked out, and Ma turned us toward the exit without even a goodbye to the Il-Cazzo's. An older man, balding, with glasses, a bit grouchy, and a lady about Ma's age, with shoulder-length dark hair, and a bright smile, motioned us toward a trolley. They took us on a short boat ride and then a bus took us to a train station in the next city. We rode away, and met two ladies in North Carolina. It took a week to reach Nebraska. I read the entire time, and thought about Vinnie.

* * *

True to my word, I attended junior high school and high school in Washington under my new last name. I kept Stephanie, I was used to it. I attended no dances or mixers. Boys showed interest, but I played it cool. I was busy anyway, with therapy, school, classes in the martial arts, and working around Doc and Billy's community. We moved to the community after three days at my grandparent's house. I wasn't comfortable around them anyway. They were severe, and kept reminding Ma that she wouldn't be in such a mess if she'd stayed home.

There were a number of veterans at the community who suffered from PTSD, and having me and Caroline around brought some of them out of their shells. Several Marines and Navy men began teaching us self defense while Ma recovered and dealt with her own trauma.

I turned back from the window, twenty-one again. Taller, supple, sinewy, and nervous. "Vinnie found me? Us? But, how?"

Doc put out his cigar, approached, and hugged me. "The internet doesn't allow for secrets, kid. I believe he tracked down your grandparents, and from there found you."

"Where is he?"

"Room 318 in the main building. We didn't confirm your presence. He said use the secret knock if you're still interested in seeing him. Otherwise, he'll move on in the morning."

"Like Hell he's moving on. I waited for him." I hugged Ma and Caroline, executed a one handed vault over the porch railing, and sprinted to the building and up the steps. I knocked 1-3-

2. The man who answered, and a man he was, looked worn out. He was still muscular, powerful, ruggedly handsome, but life had taken a toll. He was dressed in beat up boots, cheap jeans, and a faded t-shirt.

The rest of this, I choose not to tell. We had been forced apart at twelve, and I had said I wanted for a better setting than a family restroom. The community was the best setting I could ask for. We spent the next six months exploring the grounds, and each other. We were both done running.

Nick'n Nick
Terry Groves
Canada

"Get him," Nick commanded as the fat man backed away from the fireplace. A huff escaped him when Chris pulled the pillowcase over his head. The man dropped the bag he was carrying. Nick's arms circled the man's body, pinning his elbows to his sides.

"Hold him." Chris said. The man struggled to free himself. He pulled side to side, straining against the arms that held him, but Nick was two hundred and sixty pounds strong.

"Get him into the chair." Noel tugged the man's belt, pulling him backward. The man tripped over Nick's feet and sat down with a thump into the waiting chair; its high back and ornate arms resembling a throne.

"Tie him." Nick released his grip just long enough to move behind the chair and then re-pinned the man's arms to his sides with the chair back between them.

"With what?" Chris swiveled his head, looking for something that looked like a rope.

"Use that wire," Nick pointed toward the window, "Use some of that long crap on the table there."

"Oh yeah, and there's tons of stringy stuff in the other room, near the tree, that we can use too." Chris' face brightened and his eyes widened.

The fat man shook his head and strained

against Nick, but Nick was built like a bear and was just as strong. Chris ran to the window while Noel headed into the other room. Three minutes and a bag-full of curses later, the three teenagers stepped back in awe. The fat man was secured to the chair. The white trim of his clothing changed hues in time with the flashing lights that helped bind him. His red suit was perfect contrast to the gold and silver twinkly garland. A satin ribbon completed the picture, making him look like a large, elaborate Christmas present. It was fitting, Noel, Chris and Nick had successfully kidnapped Santa Claus.

Santa looked at each of the three young men standing in front of him. He stared right in their eyes. Only Nick didn't look away.

"You boys know what you've done?"

"Friggin' right we do," Chris had stepped behind Nick during the stare-down but now poked his head out of cover. "We've got you." Chris finished up with a quick giggle then looked up at Nick.

"I'm a busy man Nick. What do you want so I can be on my way?" Nick's head snapped up at the mention of his name. "Yes," Santa continued, "I know each of you. Nick, Noel, Chris"

Red flared in Chris' cheeks as he spoke, "Tell him Nick. Tell him what we want." Chris' brow wrinkled and his mouth twisted a bit as he looked up at the larger teen.

Nick coughed and shifted his weight to his other foot. He used his elbow to push Chris' face back behind him. He looked back at Chris for a moment. "What we want..." he started then paused for a moment as he shifted his weight again. "What we want is...we haven't been treated fair lately for Christmas. We want to set the record straight."

"Yeah," Chris spoke as soon as Nick stopped. The 'yeah' came out with a stutter, as though he was laughing while he said it. He clipped the little laugh and his sneer softened as he turned to look at Nick. "We want the record straight." His voice had lowered in volume as he turned back to Santa.

"And you think kidnapping me is the way to do that?"

"It'll get us heard. That's for sure."

"Sometimes getting heard in the wrong way is worse than being ignored," Santa stared at each young man in turn, fixing them with a stare that let them know he wasn't all ho-ho-ho. There was some hard-hard-hard in the man who traveled the whole world in one night each year. "Alright, you got my attention. Talk."

"Take us off your naughty list." Nick said, crossing his arms and puffing up his chest.

"Who said you were on it?" Santa asked, "Before tonight." He added after a brief pause.

"Must be." Noel grinned. "I didn't get no presents I wanted last year."

"Let's see," Santa turned his eyes to the ceiling, "You asked for a motorcycle, a trip to Mexico, and a bottle of whiskey, last year. "

"He is Santa Claus." Noel stared with wide eyes. Nick pushed him back with one big hand.

"Shut up you idiot." Nick looked at Santa, "He didn't get none of those things."

"I need a hand free if you want an answer."

"Free a hand? You think I'm stupid."

"No, I can't remember everything. I need my communication contraption."

"Your what?" Chris said but it came out 'yer whot'

"My cellular, my Cranberry. I need to get at it if you want details."

"A Cranberry? What's that? Nick asked.

"You use a Blackberry, I use a Cranberry." Santa spread the fingers of both hands.

"Forget it. You are going to take us off the naughty list and then we'll let you go."

"You realize that delaying me tonight is tantamount to being on the naughty list for a long time."

"Nope, deal is, you get us off the naughty list permanent and we let you go."

"Look boys," Santa's eyes softened, a smile pulled at his cheeks, "it doesn't work like that. I can't just take you off one of my lists, you have to earn any list jumping."

"Crapola, you're Santa and you can do anything." Chris stated with the conviction of a child.

"What makes you think that? I may be Santa, but I put my boots on one foot at a time, just like you."

"You got reindeer that fly." Noel stated.

"You got the Internet but that don't make you wise." Santa's brow furled.

"Alright, enough." Nick raised his voice and slashed the air with his arms as though he could knock the words on to the floor. "Noel saved the Jenkins kids from that house fire."

"Sure did," Noel hooked his thumb at himself, "I even got in the paper for it. Called me a h-e-r-o. That's gotta be worth something."

"Free one hand; I really need my Cranberry now." Santa asked. "I promise, no funny business."

"He promised, Nick." Noel said, "You know Santa can't lie so we can untie his hand."

"Alright," Nick said after a moment, "one

hand."

Santa reached under the hem of his
jacket, a task made difficult by the bulk of his
middle and the lights and garland that held him
in the chair. He grunted as he leaned over to one
side. He pulled his hand out and Nick heard the
snap of leather on leather, the same sound he
had heard from his father's smart phone as he
would snap it out of his belt carrier to check for
email or answer the phone.

Santa held the device in front of his face
as he squinted at the screen. Lights flickered and
danced around the edge of the red device. "Need
my specs.' Santa looked up at Nick after holding
the phone at various distances from his face,
twisting his eyes and sticking out his tongue,
trying to focus on the screen. "Inside pocket"
Santa pointed his chin at his chest. Nick reached
in and pulled out wire framed glasses with round
lenses. He unfolded them and placed them on
Santa's face.

"Lets see now,' Santa's thumb moved
quick over the keys, "Ah, here it is; yes, Noel
saves kids.' Noel smiled wide as Santa's thumb
rolled a berry shaped trackball. Then the device
emitted a flat, farting sound.

"Hmmm," Santa produced in a deep
rumble. "What they didn't know was that that fire
started from a cigarette butt you tossed into the

trash."

Noel's smile faded as Santa's words sunk in. "It was out."

"Sorry son, it wasn't. You caused that fire." Santa stared at the teen who could only look at the floor, his head moving side to side as the memory of the evening returned and the realization of what he'd done sunk in.

"But you did the right thing," Santa's smile echoed the spirit in his voice "you didn't run away, you got the boys out and called 9-1-1."

"I started the fire." Noel gleaned a look at Santa. His face twisted and he turned away.

"What about you?" Santa looked at Chris "Why should you be on the good list?"

"I kept a kid from getting run over. I ran right out and pulled him from in front of that car." Chris's eyes flicked toward Nick then back to Santa. His chin jutted out.

Santa looked at his Cranberry again and his thumb danced over the keys and spun the trackberry. "How did the boy get into the street?"

"He chased a toy."

"How did the toy get there?"

"I guess it bounced there". Chris looked down.

"You guess?" Santa said

"All right, it did. It bounced there by accident."

"Accident?"

"I didn't mean it to happen." Chris' shoulders slumped. "I did a three-pointer shot and then it bounced into the street. He should have known better than to chase it."

"Known better." Santa peered over his glasses. Chris looked at the toe of his shoe as he tried to dig a hole in the floor big enough to jump into.

"And you Nick"

"Well, there was a kid in a window." Nick paused, looked at Santa's thumb poised over the Cranberry keyboard then added, "forget it.'"

Santa stared at each boy in turn. His survey glance was long and slow and, as his eyes turned to each, the boys seemed to shrink a little. Santa took a deep breath and let it out in a rush. The lines in his face loosened and a light glinted in his eyes. He looked at his Cranberry which zinged and crackled, then back at the young men.

"I see more here." The boys took a step back. "Noel, you never hang with your friends on Sunday. Why's that?"

Noel looked up, his mouth moving but no words coming out. After a moment he managed to say, "I got stuff to do."

"Like what?'

"He has to see his probation officer."

Nick blurted.

"Is that right?" Santa continued to stare at Noel.

"Sort of." Noel took a quick glance at Nick then back at his feet.

"Sort of?"

"I always wondered what sort of proby worked on Sunday." Chris said. "None of mine ever did."

"Yours?" Santa's left eyebrow rose in a sharp arc.

"I almost had one once". Chris glanced at Santa, Noel, Nick, then went back to studying the floor.

"You were saying about Sunday." Santa returned his gaze to Noel.

"Alright.' Noel's shoulders sagged. He propped them up by jamming his fists in his pockets. "It's not my proby." He sighed then the words rushed out of him. "It's my Gram. I take her to church. She can't go by herself, she's old, and no one else in my stupid family will even talk to her. I take her because she's my gram and she has no one else." Noel's voice cracked on the last words. His eyes filled with water, but he turned away from his friends, rubbing his nose on his shoulder while red crept up his neck, flowering his cheeks. "She doesn't always remember my name, but I still love her." He peeked at Nick with a side glance.

Nick looked at Noel for a long second. Chris snickered and raised a hand to his mouth cutting it off at 'snic'. Nick snapped his head to stare hard at Chris, sealing the 'ker' forever. He looked back at Noel.

"Man, that is so cool Noel." Nick's eyes softened and he raised a hand to Noel's shoulder. Noel looked at him.

"Really? You don't think it's sucky?"

"Wish I had my Nana still. Maybe I can go with you some time?" Nick gave the shoulder a little shake.

"Sure," Noel straightened up, his chest sticking out a bit, his shoulders back and square, "any time."

"Ahem." Everyone turned back to Santa. Santa looked at each then stared at Chris. "What's your story?"

"What do you mean?" Came out waddaya mean

"What do you keep from your friends?"

"Nothing."

"Nothing," Santa aped him. "Tell us about Ron."

"These guys know Ron," Nodding heads confirmed Chris' words.

"And your dad?"

"He hates me." Chris closed his lips so

tight they became just a thin line across his face.

"Does he now?!" Santa tipped his head forward.

"He's always on me."

"Seems to me he's always on Ron."

After a moment where the gaze that existed between Santa and Chris could have been used to hang wet laundry on, Chris spoke. "I don't know why he's always so mad at Ron."

"But what do you do?"

"I just try to ease things between them."

"You really just deflect your dad's attention? Chris, I 'm Santa, you can't fool me."

"Alright, I do. If dad's mad at me he leaves Ron alone."

"How does that help?"

"He never hits me as hard." Chris' voice grew faint. Nick and Noel had to lean toward him to hear his words.

"You protect your big brother."

"It's not his fault." Chris glared at Santa. His nose had begun to run, and his eyes were red. He wiped an arm across his face. "Why are you doing this to us?"

"Seems to me you guys trapped me."

Santa turned to Nick, "Your turn young man."

"Me? I ain't got no secrets." He glanced at his two friends, at Santa, then down. He found something on the floor to keep his eyes busy.

The cranberry flashed and Nick blurted "I don't do good in school."

"And why's that?" silver eyebrows arched up.

"Cuz I'm dumb, I guess. Just don't get the numbers and letters." His words came out as more of a question than a statement.

"Nope." Santa didn't even glance at the device in his hand. "You couldn't be the leader of your little group and be stupid; and you're smart enough to know you can't slip one by me. Maybe you can fool your teachers but not me."

"I don't do homework, don't study, got better things to do."

Santa had turned his head to one side as Nick spoke and now looked at him with only one eye. "That's partly true Nick, you're smart enough to craft your words so why do you fail simple English tests?'

Nick shrugged his shoulders, looking for whatever Chris had found so interesting on the floor.

"Look at me Nick."

Nick did, studying the lines in the face of the man who brought happiness to kids all over the world.

"Tell me about your sister." A cinder snapped in the fireplace, a veritable gunshot in the silence that followed the old man's words. Nick looked at Santa then glanced at his two friends, but just a quick one, not meeting their eyes. Then he turned back to their captive. His lower lip quivered and then drew taught. His eyes firmed up.

"Untie him." The words were not a request and Noel stepped forward in instant obedience. "Let him go." Nick stormed away.

"Wait," Santa stood up, his bonds falling away as though they were overcooked spaghetti. Noel's mouth fell open. Santa looked at him a moment. "I'd be in real trouble if a little tinsel and ribbon could slow me down." Then his voice raised taking on the same tone as Nick's order to release him. "You started this son. I know you're strong enough to finish it."

"I'm not strong," Nick spun around and faced the red coated man square on, "I'm not even strong enough to hold a baby. She's feeble and it's because of me. I dropped her, now I got to protect her."

Noel and Chris both watched Nick as he spoke, his words coming short and clipped and clear. All evidence of his drawl gone, kept in by his taught lips and clenched teeth.'

"Now we get to the truth." Santa smiled but he held Nick's store, "Now we see the real Nick."

Tears cascaded down Nick's cheeks. He made no attempt to hide them. He wiped one hand across his face, wiping away the moisture. His eyes fixed on Santa as though they could pin him into the chair like the garland had been expected to. Santa sat back down but his eyes remained soft under Nick's hard glare.

"All right," Nick's shoulders sagged, "I've blown a few tests on purpose."

"A few," Chris laughed through a twisted smile. "Dude, you've failed three times. No one fails anymore."

"Sally does," Nick's words shot across the room, "'she can't keep up with everyone else, even with her Helper. Everyone picks on her, laughs at her. She cries at night."

Nick sucked in a long breath, puffed out his chest and squared his shoulders. "But not when I'm around. They know I'd kick their asses"

"And that helps?" Santa asked.

"On her good days, she dances, and it's beautiful." Nick smiled, all the anger in his face slipping away, the angles becoming curves.

"You can't be there for her forever."

"I made her into her forever."

"You were five Nick. You didn't drop her, she squirmed and slipped. You weren't responsible."

"Someone has to be responsible." The angles rushed back into Nick's face. "This frigging world don't care, won't cut her no slack."

"Maybe if you just help her dance, she can do the rest herself."

"She does dance nice," Noel spoke soft, "I've seen her."

"If you destroy your own future, you'll destroy hers too."

Nick stared hard at Santa; his lower lip moved a bit but whatever words poised on his tongue remained there. "You know the feeling when a semi-truck speeds by you, kinds of sucks you along with it?"

Heads nodded.

"And you know what it's like to be stuck behind a big truck going up a long hill?"

More nods.

"Well Nick, you're a semi and Sally is a little car. The only choice you got to make is how fast you're gonna go. Pull her along or block her way."

"By treating her special I'm hurting her?"

Now it was Santa's turn to stare in silence. After a moment light returned to his face, his smile illuminated as he raised his hands. "Boys, we got a problem."

Three faces turned to him.

"We're in trouble." Noel stated.

"I'm in trouble.' Santa corrected him. "I'm behind schedule and a lot of people are counting on me. A couple of smart lads could get me back on track, know any?"

"Not really," Nick said, a smile pulling the hard lines of his face into curves, "but us three can work like speeding Mac trucks."

"Merry Christmas lads, you boys are all right."

Running in the sun
Nick Gerrard

When that bell went we ran, we ran as fast as we could, ignoring the stitches in our sides, swinging our bags through the air...

Panting excitedly at the door.

'Mum! It's...the...holidays! No...more...school!'

The summer holidays had begun 1960's Birmingham.

Our dads' only had two weeks off from the factories so it was up to our mums' to entertain us. We were about 60 miles from the sea so it was easy to get to, though the Wales and nearby coast was freezing and we always wanted to go further south to warmer waters. But that cost money. So, Wales or Weston-Super-Mare it was.

Wales was known for its terrible weather; wind that blew sand to scrub your face, and sometimes days of lashing rain.

I remember one morning on Shell Island; I dozed and rocked in a floating dreamy feeling. I woke and was rocking, as my blow up bed floated on a foot of flood water.

So we preferred Weston. Though it was a poor first choice.

Weston was famous for the sea not being around much. You had to catch it. Be there at the right time. But most days all you saw was a vast expanse of dirty sand, the sea a dot on the horizon. Still we enjoyed playing in the mud, digging for shells or worms.

The deal was that the whole family went for two weeks then the fathers returned home. This was good for everyone. The fathers were free from kids and wives back home for 5 days until returning at the weekends. We don't know what they got up to, but we guessed it involved a lot of drinking. They looked worn out when they pitched up late Friday night.

The mums were left at the campsite with all the other mums and kids. We kids amused ourselves mainly; huge football games of thirty or more, exploring old war bunkers that smelled of piss and had ripped pieces of porn mags strewn about. We were a bit far from the beach, so we only went there once or twice a week. So we messed around in the camp pool, which never got hot and the amount of blooded heads on the kids testified to the care they had taken in building the concrete minefield surrounding the water.

The mums' of course were happy; no men around. We kids came back to be fed usually with a stew and then went off again. Appearing now and then for cash for an ice lolly or some sweets. So, the women lay around, grabbing some rays and smoking and drinking a lot. They gathered in big packs on various sun beds or camping seats and smoked and drank and bitched; but mostly we noticed they laughed. They didn't seem to do that much at home. And when I say laugh, I mean howls of laughter. We didn't know what they were laughing at and when we tried to sneak up and listen we were sent away with a swear word warning or a stick flung at your head.

Most summers went on like this, eight weeks camping, and we loved it because we were basically left to do what we wanted; we smoked and showed off our private parts to each other in the bunkers. We only saw our mums to be fed with the usual camping stew or money and then to go to bed, happy to go to sleep after an exhausting day. We lay on the camp beds and listened to the crickets and the gangs of women still laughing their heads off.

Our dads visits involved a dads vs. kids game of footy or cricket, some swimming then off to the clubhouse at night, bingo and some jiving for the grown-ups, and crisps and pop for the kids sat in a long line on the wall outside swinging their legs happily.

But some summers we went on a family journey. This involved Grandparents and uncles, aunts and cousins, all in a long caravan of second hand cars towing trailers of camping gear. These I loved the best as we ventured into deepest

Devon and farthest Cornwall. Interesting fishing villages with tiny lanes and gorgeous fish and chip suppers and tasty pasties.

We stayed on campsites for about two days then moved on. We stopped at places on the way. Hills to climb, views to be seen, ruins to be explored. We ventured into pastures unknown. I remember one time we had to go through field after field with signs warning of bulls and threats to close the gates. I was pushed out to open the gates and every car that passed me paid through the window for the favour and my valour.

The one year they decided to go on a big trip, through France to Spain. This was unheard of in those days. Working class people never went abroad; this was back before the mass package holidays and flights. I don't remember France much, we raced on through. But we arrived in Barcelona and when you look at the pictures and old cine films they took they looked like a group of bohemians. All dressed in their finery on the Ramblas...the working class of Brum, living the good life. One photo has my nan looking like Sophia Loren in pink sunglasses and a flowing flowery dress sat on a bench in Parc Guel; behind her my granddad stands proudly looking like Rudolph Valentino in his suit trousers and open necked shirt, greased back hair and pencil moustache. The campsite was not too far from the city. So we explored the lanes and avenues experiencing new smells and sounds; we felt like in a kid's adventure book.

And the sea! The sea was warm! And the sand was too hot for your feet, so we bought flip-flops and felt elegant. The food was weird. Rice with sea food, which we hesitantly picked at, at first, but grew to love, and meat on sticks from smoking grills, which we wolfed down. Our parents drank wine in the circle of chairs in the middle of the tents into the dark of night. I got ill, some bug or something. And I had a fever and felt like I was in a dream I was carried into a hospital and remember this evil doctor with some metal thing on his head evilly grinning at me muttering in words like Tolkien's elves and his gold tooth sparkling in my dreary eyes as he bore down on me with a huge needle; then I floated off into a world of seas, ice-creams and running...I saw myself running and laughing in the sun; never-ending running on the sand...until I woke.

Printed in Great Britain
by Amazon

56076892R00144